Ro

Narrative of the Late War in New Zealand

SALZWASSER
VERLAG

Robert Carey

Narrative of the Late War in New Zealand

Reprint of the original, first published in 1863.

1st Edition 2022 | ISBN: 978-3-37500-128-5

Verlag (Publisher): Salzwasser Verlag GmbH, Zeilweg 44, 60439 Frankfurt, Deutschland
Vertretungsberechtigt (Authorized to represent): E. Roepke, Zeilweg 44, 60439 Frankfurt, Deutschland
Druck (Print): Books on Demand GmbH, In de Tarpen 42, 22848 Norderstedt, Deutschland

NARRATIVE

OF

THE LATE WAR

IN

NEW ZEALAND

BY

LIEUTENANT-COLONEL CAREY. C.B.

DEPUTY-ADJUTANT-GENERAL

LONDON

1863

CONTENTS.

CHAPTER I.

CHAPTER II.

CHAPTER III.

CHAPTER III.—*continued.*

CHAPTER IV.

CHAPTER V.

CHAPTER VI.

CHAPTER VI.—*continued.*

CHAPTER VII.

CHAPTER VIII.

CHAPTER IX.

THE WAR IN NEW ZEALAND

IN

1860–1861.

CHAPTER I.

Origin of the war — Military force on the island — Martial law proclaimed — Operations confined to the Taranaki district — Arrival of reinforcements from Australia — Commencement of hostilities.

I PROPOSE in the following pages to give a brief narrative of the events of the New Zealand war of 1860–1861, in the Taranaki district, so far as the military operations under Major-General Pratt are concerned.

It is not my intention, nor would it become me, to enter on the justice or policy of the quarrel. These considerations belong more especially to those whose duty it has been to investigate that portion of Mäori history, which discusses native title to land, and the proper interpretation of our treaties with the natives.*

I shall, therefore, only slightly touch upon the origin of the war, and confine myself principally to the military operations of the troops, under the command of Major-General Pratt—commencing in August 1860—by which the war was brought to a successful termination in March 1861.

The unsettled appearance of European politics, the supposed increase of the French force in New Caledonia, and other circumstances, had for some time caused attention to be drawn to the small military and naval forces in the Australian colonies,

* The Government despatches, and others referred to, will be found in Parliamentary papers on New Zealand, presented to Parliament in March 1861, and at the pages as here noted in the margin.

and to the great interests there at stake. Some of these colonies—and Victoria in particular—had made most expensive preparations for self-defence.

In addition to these external causes of anxiety, New Zealand had an internal disturbing element of its own to guard against, in its Mäori inhabitants of the northern island, who were numerous, warlike, and independent, and who, though living nominally under our rule, had never acknowledged themselves a conquered race. Nor had our successes in former wars given them much reason for so doing; and while they had been willing at first to see the white man in their country, and to accept the benefits and luxuries he introduced, they had neither contemplated his soon overpowering them, and becoming the dominant race, nor had they calculated upon seeing their lands and old regal sway pass into his hands.

The probability that such results would

follow was brought prominently before them by the vain boasting of the settlers, who openly declared to these proud tribes, that, whether they liked it or not, they must sell their lands to them. While to keep this race in good temper, as much care and respect had hitherto been paid to their prejudices and habits as to those of the most high-caste Hindoo! For undeniably, for the interests of the colony and its colonists, collision with the native population was on all accounts to be avoided.

At the commencement of the year 1860, the military and naval force in the colony was particularly small: the infantry, by the withdrawal, in October 1858, of the 58th Regiment, being reduced to one regiment. The colonists were scattered over the face of the island without the slightest regard, either in the choice of their land, or of sites for their houses, to military or even to mutual defence. The country itself was a network of gullies, ravines, marshes, and impenetrable forest; and, except in the neighbourhood of the townships, destitute of roads; and even those near towns were hardly better than cart-tracks, impassable in winter.

To these matters His Excellency the Governor appears to have been fully alive, when, in March 1859, he entertained the offer of Te Teira to sell the block of land at the Waitara, which became, if not the origin, certainly the pretext for the war. For in pressing, in August of the same year, on the Secretary of State for the Colonies the danger of a foreign invasion, he adds in a despatch:—'The internal defence of the colony is, however, a difficult question; I cannot but see with some uneasiness the continuance of the movement in favour of the Mäori King. With the means at my disposal nothing can be done or could be done to ávoid it; nor do I apprehend any immediate danger from it. Should any unforeseen circumstances lead to a collision, the union of a large body of natives under a single chief, with their central position and the fastnesses of their country, would give them a great advantage.

'There are seldom wanting in New Zealand disaffected Europeans, who, for selfish purposes, desire to foment discord between the two races; and by the last mail from Wellington I learn that a deserter, and others, have been disturbing the minds of the natives in that district, and exciting them to arm; that they were purchasing arms extensively, and being drilled, and had used menaces that had alarmed the settlers and the civil authorities.

'I trust that these fears will prove exaggerated, and that the evil influence may not yet spread beyond the district. If, however, blood were once shed by the Europeans, even in self-defence, it would be impossible to foresee the consequences. Some defenceless family would be murdered in revenge. The murderers would find countenance and support in their tribe; and the flame of war, once kindled, would extend through the whole island.

'There can be no doubt of the ultimate success of Her Majesty's arms in any contest with the native race; but the consequences to the scattered European population of the colony of even a successful conflict could not but be ruinous and distressing in the extreme.'

This opinion, so strongly expressed, cannot but have been the firm conviction of all the thinking portion of the community, who had at heart not only their personal interests, but the general good of the colony which they had adopted as their home.

But though the colonists held much more land than they did or could cultivate, still land was the cry of the greedy; and whenever a rich tract, cultivated or uncultivated, came under their notice, they considered themselves entitled to insist on the purchase of it by the Government (and subsequent sale to them), whether the native owner desired to part with his property or not.

Thus the Governor, who virtually, under the new constitution, has little power, may have found himself compelled to take the course he adopted by the political pressure brought to bear on him by interested parties. Possibly he was deceived by the misrepresentation of facts, and by exaggerated and partial statements, more especially of those who insisted on the ease with which, with a show of determination, the desideratum could be obtained; and he was therefore, perhaps, driven to yield to the cry, and to agree to the purchase of an insignificant block of land; and thus, although he strongly deprecated any resort to arms to bring to an issue the question of the native king movement, which, in his despatch of August 1859, he states he has not means at his disposal to resist.

No greater proof need be required that

both the quarrel itself, and the time selected for it, were of our own seeking, and that the issue might have been postponed until a more convenient season, than the tardiness with which the more powerful and influential tribes implicated themselves in large numbers in it, and the extreme caution with which they avoided being the first to shed blood. Our own acts left them no choice. They were driven either to take up William King's quarrel, or to give up the native king movement; and it was not likely that the proud and independent Waikato would take this latter course.

The territory in which the land in question lay had long been a bone of contention, and the legal title to it by Te Teira, the native possessor, a doubtful point. This chief, however, at the instigation of interested Europeans, who coveted the land, and contrary to the wish of his own people, and particularly of William King—who claimed a right of sovereignty over it, and power to forbid its sale (and this he did in a most insulting manner)—offered, in March 1859, to dispose of the property. The Governor consented to buy it, if the seller could prove his title. Te Teira appears to have done so; for in January 1860, the purchase was ordered to be completed.

Here it may be remarked, that New Zealand treaties provided that all land should be sold, in the first instance, by the Mäori to the Government, who retailed it to the settlers; and that no land should be bought unless the settler could prove indefeasible right to the property.

Since the reduction of troops in the island in 1858, and during all 1859, and until March 1860, the whole military force in New Zealand consisted of Royal Artillery, Royal Engineers, and the 65th Regiment, in all about 1,000 rank and file, and distributed thus:—

Auckland	400
Wellington	100
Wanganui	200
Napier	120

and those in the Taranaki district, stationed at New Plymouth, twelve miles from the seat of the dispute, who numbered only:—

	Captains	Subalts.	Sergeants	Rank and File
Royal Artillery . .	—	—	1	6
Royal Engineers . .	—	—	1	4
65th Regiment . .	2	3	11	182
Total . . .	2	3	13	192

In January 1860, the purchase was ordered to be made, and, as affairs looked far from settled, His Excellency furnished Captain and Bt. Lieut.-Colonel Murray, 65th Regiment, at that time in command at New Plymouth, with certain instructions as to the course he should pursue, in the event of opposition being offered to the surveyors sent to complete the sale, and entrusted to him a proclamation of martial law,* to be used if requisite. The survey and the actual taking possession of the land was not at this time begun, and matters remained in this unsatisfactory state, even becoming worse, until the 11th February, when Colonel Murray wrote to Auckland, recommending that he should be supplied with a small reinforcement of 50 men, in case he should have to move to the Waitara. On the 20th of the same month he wrote to William King, that Mr. Parris, the native commissioner, sent down to complete the purchase, had reported that the surveyors had been interrupted, and that they could not carry on their duties; and that this interruption by his tribe was an overt act of rebellion: he warned him of the consequence of persist-

* Proclamation of martial law is interpreted by the natives to mean a declaration of war. Power to call out the militia for service was also at this time ted to Colonel Murray.

ing in this course, and gave him till the 22nd to reflect on the matter; and on that day William King, not having given a satisfactory reply to this communication, he put in force the proclamation of martial law entrusted to him in January previous.

Though the natives had committed themselves to an act of rebellion against the Queen, they had done it in a very cautious and innocuous manner. Some stones had been thrown at the surveyors, and some old women had taken up the end of the chain, and had interfered with the performance of their work. But no blood had been shed; and the natives at this time, and ever after, declared that the step they had taken was in no hostility to the Queen of England, but was in defence of their own lands, which they maintained we were forcing unjustly from them in an unprecedented manner, in defiance of existing treaties. In this opinion, as to the justice of their cause, they were strongly supported by the clergy, as well as by a large and influential portion of the community generally, and they would have been supported by others also, had not personal interests been concerned in the possession of the coveted land. The effect of this division of opinion among the European population acted most prejudicially on the native mind, as is well shown in a speech attributed to a native, who, after the termination of the war in March 1861, is reported to have said, in a conversation at Auckland, 'How can you expect the Waikato to give up his king movement, when half your own council are for it?'

The antagonistic views held by our people, and their unguarded and impolitic expression, enhanced greatly the difficulties surrounding the Governor; led the natives to believe that he would be obliged to yield the point in dispute; and tended greatly to foster the growing disaffection among the tribes. William King, at a later period, by putting the piece of land at the disposal of the native king, obliged the Waikato to espouse his (W. King's) quarrel, or to resign the king movement. The latter could not be expected. But in taking the former course, the Waikato was understood to have entered into at least a tacit if not an express agreement with the Government, that the quarrel should be kept in the Taranaki district, and that all fighting should be there alone. This singular arrangement remained virtually in force until the end of the war in March 1861. It was an excellent one for the natives. They had gained the choice of a battle-field in a country most difficult to Europeans, and favourable to themselves. They had selected a spot distant from their own homes and cultivations, where they had nothing to lose but life. It was a most central position for the union of their tribes. But yet it was not without its advantage to us; for, as long as we could depend on the natives keeping to the agreement, it saved the ruin of the other exposed provinces; and it enabled the officer in command at the time, who had not men nor means at his disposal for general offensive operations, to adopt the views of the Governor, which were to endeavour to overawe the native mind by the greatest display of the small military force at his command. And subsequently—some months after—by confining the war to this district, pending the arrival of reinforcements, it enabled Major-General Pratt, instead of breaking up his small army for the defence of our widely-scattered settlements in the northern island, at that time left with most inadequate garrisons, to carry out a well-digested plan of operations, with his increased though still inadequate force. By repeated and unvaried successes over the enemy, in this their chosen seat of operations, he was enabled heartily to disgust them with a war in which they got nothing but hard blows, and which compelled them to send back to Waikato hosts of maimed, besides, according to their own confession, leaving above 400 of their best and bravest dead upon the field, as well as abandoning the bodies of many chiefs to the Europeans; while at the same time large reinforcements and supplies were on their way from England; and preparations were being made for a general war, should an event so lamentable to the colony be unavoidable.

The news of the proclamation of martial law, and of the unsatisfactory state of affairs in the province of Taranaki, reached Auckland on the 24th February, and the Governor decided on proceeding at once to the spot with all available men.

Colonel Gold, commanding in New Zealand, embarked with about 200 men at the Manukau, on the 28th of February, and landing next day at New Plymouth, assumed the direction of military affairs. The troops at his disposal were then :—

	F. O.	Capts.	Subalts.	Sergts.	Rank and File
Royal Artillery . .	—	—	1	2	20
Royal Engineers .	—	—	1	1	10
65th Regiment . .	1	4	8	28	360

These were further strengthened by such forces from the navy as could be spared from the ships on the coast, and by the Taranaki Militia, who had been called out on proclamation of martial law, on the 22nd February.

The intimation that these steps had been taken, and that a collision had become inevitable, reached General Pratt, at Melbourne, on the 14th March 1861, in a letter dated February 26th. The terms in which the letter was worded, however, showed that no great alarm existed that hostilities would be of long duration, nor was the necessity for any reinforcement hinted at.

Colonel Murray had, indeed, on the 20th of February, in a letter addressed to the authorities in Auckland, brought under their notice the terrible consequences that might fall on the wives and families of those called on to serve in the militia, and on the want of training of the volunteers, and their numerical weakness. Of this, however, little notice was taken at the time.

On April 5th 1860, the Governor-General, Sir William Denison, telegraphed to Melbourne that he had received despatches from New Zealand conveying a demand for troops, and he expressed his willingness to spare a portion of those stationed in New South Wales, should General Pratt require them. The same patriotic course was adopted by the Governors of Victoria and the other Australian colonies, their only anxiety apparently being that reinforcements shonld be sent without delay. The colony of Victoria also placed at the disposal of the Major-General for the transport of troops, and other service that might be requisite, their fine war steam-sloop 'Victoria.'

The whole of the expense of this ship, its wear and tear, and all outlay, with the exception of coal, was borne by the colony of Victoria. From the 17th of April 1860, until her return to Melbourne, on the termination of the war, this sloop, which, from its build and steam power, was better suited for this service than any of Her Majesty's navy on the coast, rendered the most valuable assistance as a transport; while at the same time her indefatigable and ever-ready commander, Captain Norman, was always anxious to advance the interests of the State in every way, by furnishing such officers and men as he could spare for duty on shore; thus enabling them to share in the military operations of the campaign in which they rendered most effectual service.

General Pratt lost no time in complying with the demand for aid, though this demand had only reached him by telegram, and was necessarily vague and incomplete; and on the 10th April 1860, the first reinforcement, consisting of a small detachment of the 12th Regiment and of Artillery, sailed from Sydney. On the 17th, the 'City of Hobart' steamer left Melbourne with two companies of the 40th Regiment, and the 'Victoria' started for Tasmania to convey further reinforcements from that colony. These troops, besides being well supplied with camp equipage, ammunition, &c., took one month's provisions and as large a supply of stores for general service as the ships could carry.

On the 16th (the day previous to the embarkation), Colonel Gold's despatch, to which the telegram referred, arrived: it was dated 'Gore Browne Redoubt,' Waitara, March 19th, 1860. It gave no information, but simply asked for reinforcements. It, however, enclosed an important document from Mr. M'Lean, the native secretary, who saw the magnitude of the quarrel, and recommended 5,000 men at once for the defence of the colony. These letters, which had been delayed in consequence of having been forwarded through an unusual channel, were quickly followed by further despatches from Colonel Gold at New Plymouth, dated March 31st, enclosing duplicates of a despatch to the Military Secretary, Horse Guards, detailing the capture and destruction by the troops under his command, on the 18th, of a small pah that had been erected by William King's tribe on our purchased land. Some letters were still missing, and on May 28th 1860, duplicates of letters from March 6th to the 20th were received. From the earliest of these it appeared that about the 4th of March Colonel Gold had moved all the troops he could muster to the Waitara, where a camp had been selected and entrenched, and named, in honour of His Excellency, who was present at the time, 'Gore Browne Redoubt;' the name was, however, changed, on the 19th of the same month, to 'Camp Waitara.'

From these letters it appeared, too, that on the 20th of the same month, Colonel Gold urged His Excellency to demand further reinforcements from the Australian colonies, 'as their very appearance would, in all probability, induce the natives to sue for peace.' The same mail also brought a despatch from Colonel Gold at New Plymouth, dated March 26th 1860, stating that at the request of His Excellency, in consequence of the unprotected state of the town, he had gone there with a portion of the force, but had left the camp adequately protected. And another despatch, dated March 30th, stated that, on ascertaining that some families still residing at a distance on the Omata block were in danger from the natives surrounding them, he had sent a small force, consisting of military, naval brigade, and militia, to bring them in. This force came into collision with the natives at

Waireka Valley, who, with few casualties on our side, were repulsed. The immediate cause of alarm for the safety of these families was, that after the capture and destruction of William King's pah, on the 18th of the month, some Europeans had been attacked and killed by the natives on the Omata block. These fatal results Colonel Gold described as 'barbarous murders'—a term hardly applicable, however much the casualties were to be deplored, when we reflect that a guerilla warfare, in this intricate country, was the only one in which the Mäori could hope to gain any advantage, and that the acts occurred after martial law had been proclaimed by us; after we had attacked a native pah, and blood had been shed on both sides; and after these very Europeans had been warned by the natives that war having now begun, it was no longer safe for them to wander about the district.

Though the natives, in resisting the survey, had made the first overt act of rebellion, they had left it to us to commence the first act of bloodshed, by our attack on the pah on the 18th. The fact that the deaths above alluded to took place eight or ten days after our attack on this pah, was carefully kept in the background by the local papers, which tried to make it appear, and for a long time succeeded in doing so, that the Mäori had commenced the war by the murder of unarmed, unwarned, and inoffensive settlers. Whereas war having been begun by us, the natives naturally enough considered this retaliation a legitimate mode of fighting.

CHAPTER II.

Operations in the neighbourhood of New Plymouth — Attack on Puketakauere Pah repulsed by the natives — True cause of the quarrel — Native opinion of our tactics — Cause and results of the failure at Puketakauere.

IN the early part of April His Excellency returned to Auckland, whence he wrote thanks for the prompt and valuable aid sent him from Melbourne and from the other colonies; and on the 16th of May intimation was received that all the troops sent had arrived. During the first few weeks of April no movements took place at New Plymouth or at the Waitara, and the troops were only employed in furnishing escorts, collecting crops, &c.; and the Governor sanctioned the raising a company of fifty natives from the friendly tribes to aid them in these duties.

On the 20th of April Colonel Gold, anxious to afford relief to the settlers to the south of the town, organised a small column for that purpose, and moved as far as the Tartaraimaka block,* about eighteen miles distant. New Plymouth, however, was, by this withdrawal of part of the garrison, left as unprotected, that he did not think it prudent to move farther off until the 26th April, when the first detachment of the 40th Regiment arrived. Feeling the place more secure, he then pushed south as far as the Warea Pah, destroying native pahs, villages, and crops on the way; and having done all the damage he could, and not thinking it prudent to remain any longer away, he returned by the 1st of May,

* The word *block* is used in New Zealand to designate a portion of land purchased at a particular time, and opened to settlement: thus, the Omata block, the Bell block, the Grey block, &c.

leaving a military post on the Tartaraimaka block.

On the 14th of May, Colonel Gold wrote to His Excellency, urging on him the necessity of his being furnished with specific instructions regarding the operations against William King, as the approach of winter rendered all further delay dangerous. To this he received His Excellency's reply, dated Auckland, 17th May:—

'The operations at Taranaki are of minor importance to those which must ensue if the Waikato tribes take part in the war. I have, therefore, to request that you will abstain, until you hear from me again, from all interference with William King, unless he should himself commence hostilities.

'Should he do so, I recommend your offering a free passage to any of the Waikato tribe who, being with him, may be willing to leave his pahs.

'Your not having attacked the pah in the south, as described by Mr. Reimenschneider, appears to me to have been very judicious; and I am not aware that anything more can be done to punish the Taranaki and Ngatiruanui tribes; but should you find an opportunity you will, of course, not neglect it.'

And on the 31st March His Excellency wrote to General Pratt:—

'The disaffection which commenced at New Plymouth has spread through the more powerful tribes that reside in the Waikato, and it is not possible to form any satisfactory opinion of the future. At the present moment the aspect of affairs is threatening. My wish has been to confine military operations to the province of New Plymouth as much as possible, and, in order to do so, Auckland should be placed in such a state of defence as to offer no temptations for an attack; at present this is not the case, for the garrison consists of untrained militia, partially armed, some volunteers, and about fifty men of the 65th Regiment, available for duty.'

Enclosed with this letter was one from Mr. M'Lean, reporting matters as looking gloomy—large native meetings having been held, and declarations having been made of throwing off Her Majesty's allegiance; and adding:—

'I do not apprehend any immediate move on the part of the natives, unless some insult or attack is made upon their people about Auckland or elsewhere. The force applied for will not be sufficient to bring them under subjection of the British law and authority.'

On the 14th and 16th of July letters from Colonel Gold reached Melbourne. In these he reported that nothing had taken place up to the 23rd of June, in consequence of His Excellency having requested him not to move against William King, for political reasons, involving the rising of some of the largest tribes in the neighbourhood of Auckland and other posts denuded of troops.

The troops in the Taranaki district now amounted to 1,700; of these, 600 were militia and volunteers; they occupied an extended line of posts, the largest of which was under the command of Major Nelson, 40th Regiment, at the camp Waitara, which consisted of a few Royal Artillery, Royal Engineers, and about 300 of the 40th Regiment.

On the 23rd of June the commanding officer at the Waitara reported to New Plymouth that, having reason to believe that some of William King's tribe, who held Puketakauere (a pah on native land about 2,000 yards distant from our camp), were trespassing on our purchased block, he had sent out a reconnoitring party, which, on its return, was followed by the natives; that when it neared the Waitara camp it was fired on by the enemy, who at this time were, it was presumed, on our land, and that then, and not till then, were the troops directed to fire.

Some further correspondence took place on the 24th and 25th, and on the 26th the Brigade-Major wrote to Major Nelson, by direction of Colonel Gold, as follows:—

'In consequence of the representations contained in your letter of yesterday's date, I am directed by the Colonel Commanding to inform you that he sends down by the "Tasmanian Maid" an augmentation to your force, as per margin; and he trusts that with them you will be enabled to teach these troublesome natives a lesson they will not easily forget.

'You will be pleased to take every necessary precaution against the wily foe, as regards ambuscades, which the friendly natives would be the best to discover; as also, if possible, cut off their retreat. From the elevated position of the rebels a good view can be obtained of your camp, which must remain amply garrisoned, all remaining on duty armed and accoutred.

'I have caused ample information to be afforded to Captain Richards, 40th Regiment, and Lieut. Macnaughten, R.A., and I am directed to add that Colonel Gold, from your former experience, relies confidently on your proceedings.'

This letter as it reached Melbourne was incomplete, the strength of the reinforcements having been omitted in the margin. The addition, however, was some of the 40th Regiment and Naval Brigade, enabling Major Nelson, leaving what he considered sufficient for the defence of the camp, to detail the following for an attack on the enemy's position:—

	F. O.	Capts.	Subalts	Sergts.	Rank and File
Royal Artillery . .	—	—	1	—	20
Royal Engineers .	—	—	1	—	6
Naval Brigade . .	1	—	3	—	50
40th Regiment . .	1	3	5	—	245
Royal Marines . .	—	—	1	—	10
Total . .	2	3	11	—	331

At daybreak on the 27th of June this small force, in three divisions, moved to the attack of the enemy's pah. The action commenced at 7 A.M., and notwithstanding the bravery of the officers and men engaged they were completely defeated, and retreated into the camp, which they gained at half-past 11 A.M., with a loss of thirty—missing, killed, or wounded, left on the field, and thirty-two wounded, who were conveyed to the camp.

The news of this severe disaster was first made known at Melbourne, by telegraph from Sydney, on the 12th July; and without waiting for further news an additional reinforcement was sent from Sydney.

The Major-General in command decided on proceeding at once to the seat of war, and taking every available man from the other colonies. The Head-quarters of the 40th Regiment embarked at Melbourne on the 18th, and on the 24th the General and staff sailed in the 'Victoria.'

The colonies were now quite denuded of troops, and in Victoria the garrison duties were done by the volunteer force.

The Head Quarters, 40th Regiment, reached New Plymouth on July 31st, and the Major-General landed on the 3rd August 1860, from which time he took personal direction of the war.

In the above account I have been compelled to avoid going into detail as to the operations themselves, and as to the mode in which they were conducted; partly because my information on these subjects at a distance was meagre, and partly because the many various statements of the occurrences precluded any true notions being arrived at, without an investigation, for which there was no time or means, while the war lasted. Moreover I have since heard that a court of enquiry has been sitting to enquire into some of these matters. And also my object hitherto has been simply to point out clearly the chain of events and their results, which brought affairs to the crisis in which they were on the 3rd of August 1860.

At the outbreak in February 1860, the native tribes opposed to us were, William King's at the Waitara, and the Taranaki and Ngatiruanui tribes at the south—men whom the Waikato looked down on as slaves, and whom our own people acknowledged as an inferior race, in customs, independence, build, and courage to the Waikato and other tribes that shortly joined in the fight.

The capture of the pah on the 18th of March, and the skirmish at the Waireka, were in themselves of too little consequence to affect materially the general quarrel, which, though not yet fully developed, clearly did not originate in the purchase of a block of 600 acres of land, but in the question as to the right of the chief of the tribe to allow or forbid the sale. The very exaggerated view we took of the importance of these two skirmishes, and our public boasting of them, tended greatly to lower our military character; and the means and appliances for conquest at our disposal seemed small in the eyes of the more warlike native tribes, who openly expressed their surprise that so much should be thought of these events, and plainly declared that the fighting they meant would be a very different and much more serious matter.

The march to the south as far as the Warea pah (though the only move, apparently, that Colonel Gold could make) was, with the exception of saving some furniture, property, and crops, productive of no good; and by the burning of the native 'wharees' or houses, and by the destruction of deserted pahs on the road, furnished the natives with the pretext of a systematic raid on the empty and deserted stations of the settlers.

The real event of importance, and that which drove the martial spirit of the Mäori beyond the bounds of discretion or common sense, and gave great impetus to the king movement, and to the assembling of the native tribes for war, was the defeat sustained by us on the 27th June. The following extract from a letter received later during the war will show the view the natives took of the matter.

It is from a native, Tamati Ngapora:—

'September 27, 1860.

'Tamati Ngapora states that the natives engaged in the conflict at Puketakauere express their great astonishment at the mode of warfare adopted by the military, by which they continually expose themselves to great loss, though vastly superior in numbers to the natives. He says, why are not soldiers taught to fight after the native fashion? They cannot help being beaten if they continue to fight as if they were fighting Pakehas. The natives admire their personal courage, but say that it is this that causes their destruction, for they move so steadily and so close that one bullet kills two men.'

Tamati further states that the natives laugh at the idea of being taken by the soldiers, and feel fully assured that with the advantage of cover, and their knowledge of the country, they are more than a match for any number of soldiers; and that if peace is brought about, the road to it will not be fighting.

Tamati also states his conviction that if the natives continue on every occasion to beat the soldiers, as they maintain they have done, it is to be feared that the native tribes will forget their old feuds and join against us.

Tamati further adds that the number of natives actually engaged at Puketakauere, at the Waitara, has been much over-estimated, and that the number of the Waikato, exclusive of the natives of Kawhia, was 140, and of that party none were killed.

Their exclamation after the fight was one

of extreme surprise, followed by the question—How is it that we all escape?

Puketakauere itself was a strong well-built pah, fortified and garrisoned by the tribes of the district, aided by some Waikatos, fewer than were supposed at the time; but it was still well garrisoned. It was in a position difficult of access, surrounded by gullies, marshes, dense fern and brambles, and intricate and dangerous ground. Its capture, with loss to the enemy, would at this time have had a marked effect on the war; and if it had not ended it would, at all events, have deterred many tribes not yet implicated from joining in it.

In the manner in which it was undertaken it could not have succeeded without much loss on our side, while the probability was that it could not succeed at all; and if it did, the escape of the Mäori garrison could hardly have been prevented.

A small body of 300 men was divided into three parties, and sent with bad guides into an unknown, swampy, and impracticable country broken with ravines, the nature of which totally precluded the possibility of mutual support or communication. Heavy rains and the clayey soil added to the difficulties; and our troops, from the first, had no chance. The Mäori had baited the usual trap, and we walked into it.

The defeat of the troops was so signal and so complete that the Mäori declared ultimate victory over us to be in his own hands, and therefore many wavering tribes joined in the quarrel. In addition to the moral effect of this defeat, our actual loss had been so great (viz. sixty casualties, of which half, killed and wounded, left on the field, had been tomahawked and killed by the natives), that the most cautious among them felt that the time for negotiation and terms was now past, and that they were too deeply implicated to be admitted to favour without such sacrifices as they were not prepared to make. It had, in fact, been too great a success, and one greater than they hoped or wished for. Nor could the Governor now withdraw from his line of policy, or entertain propositions, until some signal and decisive success should attend our arms, and should thus compel the Mäori to acknowledge his inferiority and ask for peace.

Native emissaries carried the news of the victory all over the country, and, while admitting the bravery of the Pakeha, they laid much stress on our ignorance of the country and manner of fighting, and on the certainty of our being beaten. They thus gained many adherents to the king league.

From this date affairs remained at a standstill, and no operations were undertaken. The Europeans were confined more closely to their townships and camps, and the natives, emboldened by their success, ventured near to the town of New Plymouth by night, burnt houses, and marauded in y direction.

Colonel Gold, who then commanded, was much maligned for inactivity; but it is quite clear that, up to the 28th of June at all events, his hands were tied, and that, in allowing the attack of the day previous, he had carefully satisfied himself that the grounds on which that attack was made were supported by evidence that the enemy had fired the first shot at the reconnoitring party sent out on the 23rd. After this event no choice was left him but to await the result of his despatch to Melbourne soliciting reinforcements. Any further reverse, or even success, if attended with great loss of life on our side, would, without doubt, have crippled his small force, and would have been the ruin of all the scattered settlements in the northern island.

CHAPTER III.

Major-General Pratt arrives at New Plymouth — Number and distribution of the troops — Topography of the Taranaki district — Description of Warea Forest Pah — Strength of the enemy — Sources of information regarding their movements — Their military capabilities — Native commissariat.

On the 3rd August 1860, Major-General Pratt landed at New Plymouth, and took personal direction of the war.

The troops in the colony of New Zealand were in numbers and distribution as here shown; and out of these 860 were militia and volunteers:—

	F. O.	Capt.	Subs.	Departmental Staff	Sergts.	Drs.	Rank and File
Taranaki . .	11	29	60	23	139	44	2,320
Auckland . .	—	2	2	1	14	2	212
Napier . . .	—	2	4	1	5	2	144
Wellington .	1	5	11	—	17	1	269
Wanganui . .	1	1	3	—	10	2	187
Total . .	13	39	80	25	185	51	3,132

THE TROOPS IN THE TARANAKI DISTRICT BEING STATIONED AT THE FOLLOWING POSTS:—

	F.O.	Capts.	Subalts	Staff	Sergts.	Drs.	Rank and File	
Staff	4	2	1	—	4	—	—	
Commissariat Department	—	—	—	4	—	—	—	
Medical do.	—	—	—	3	—	—	—	
Purveyor's do.	—	—	—	1	—	—	—	
Military Store do.	—	—	—	1	—	—	—	
Royal Artillery	—	1	—	—	1	—	24	
Royal Engineers	1	2	—	—	2	—	30	New Plymouth.
40th Regiment	1	2	4	4	15	13	154	
65th Regiment	—	4	11	4	39	12	595	
Naval Brigade	2	2	10	1	8	2	169	
Militia	1	7	9	2	27	7	425	
12th Regiment	—	—	—	—	—	—	6	
Total	9	20	35	20	96	34	1,403	

	F. O.	Capts.	Subalts.	Staff	Sergts.	Drs.	Rank and File	
Royal Artillery	—	—	1	—	—	—	25	Waitara.
Royal Engineers	—	—	1	—	—	—	10	
40th Regiment	1	4	5	1	17	4	266	
Naval Brigade	—	2	6	1	5	2	141	
Militia	—	—	—	—	—	—	15	
Total	1	6	13	2	22	6	457	
Royal Artillery	—	—	—	—	—	—	3	Bell Block.
12th Regiment	—	2	4	1	7	2	119	
Militia	—	—	2	—	1	—	43	
Total	—	2	6	1	8	2	165	
Militia	—	1	—	—	3	1	49	Omata.
Royal Artillery	—	—	—	—	1	—	11	Waireka.
Royal Engineers	—	—	—	—	1	—	5	
12th Regiment	1	1	2	—	4	1	127	
40th Regiment	—	1	2	—	4	1	103	
Total	1	2	4	—	10	2	246	

This distribution was the one that was adopted by Colonel Gold when his force was too small for any operations at a distance, and when his hands were tied from attacking William King at the Waitara. It was clearly made to afford confidence to the settlers, and to encourage them to occupy their farms and cultivate their grounds, at all events in the neighbourhood of New Plymouth, and was not made with the intention of undertaking active offensive movements against the native tribes. Col. Gold's object might, to a certain degree, have been attained previous to the defeat of the 27th of June, but after that the arrangement proved totally inoperative; and by disseminating his small force over a large district, it quite precluded the assembly of a column sufficient for the field, and was of no advantage to the colonists.

To the non-military reader the effective force may appear larger than it really was; and it may be well here to remark that these numbers represent every man in the service, sick, infirm, wounded, orderlies, semaphore station-men, and others, employed on duties that necessarily devolved on the army.

The militia, numbering on paper 425, could barely muster 100 for service; except in case of an attack on the town, when each man had his appointed post. Many of them, however, made no secret of it, that if this did happen, they would stand at their own houses, and defend their families there, and not attend to orders. The militia and volunteers were the whole male population of the town capable of doing any work; consequently large numbers had to be struck off garrison duty to carry on the trades of butchers, bakers, grocers, carters, and for employment as commissariat labourers, boatmen, &c. — not only for the army but for the population of the town, now largely increased by the influx of settlers from the more distant parts of the district. Nor was it fair to expect any good service from them; they were ill armed, ill organised, and without any discipline, and had not as yet had either time or means to become an efficient auxiliary force, however anxious they might be to learn their duty.

The situation of the town of New Plymouth, and the configuration of the whole of the Taranaki district, were most adverse to military operations. The district extends on the north from the Waitara, and to the river Patea on the south. Small and divided parts of it belong to Europeans, the much larger portion to the natives—friendly, hostile, and doubtful. The town itself is on the sea-coast, twelve miles from the Waitara. Landing, only to be effected by means of surf-boats, at all times difficult and dangerous, is at many periods of the year impracticable. No master of any sailing-ship would ever stay on the coast a moment longer than absolutely necessary.

Steamers, with troops on board, had frequently to put out to sea for days until the weather moderated; and during the winter the steamers in the naval squadron on the station were kept away for as long as ten days at a time. The colonial steam-sloop 'Victoria,' which having most steam-power held her ground the longest, had on one or two occasions to put to sea, and did not return for some days.

The striking features of the place were Marsland Hill, on which were the barracks, Mount Elliot, and the Sugar Loaves. In the background, about thirty miles distant, stood Mount Egmont, 8,250 feet high, during the greater part of the year a perfect cone of snow, which, though partially melting, never during the greatest heat entirely disappears. The torrents caused by the melting snow and heavy rain rush down the sides of the deep and precipitous ravines which rise from it or from its offshoots, and which intersect the whole of this part of the district to the very coast, and even to the town of New Plymouth. Thus the ravines, which are sometimes dry and covered with furze and brambles, are at other times rapid mountain torrents, often impassable.

Difficult and adverse as this description of country was to military operations, even it did not extend above three to five miles inland, where began the interminable and impracticable forest, running nearly parallel with the coast. A better description of this forest can hardly be given than is contained in the following letter from Mr. Reimenschneider to Colonel Gold. It will be borne in mind that the country he describes is that in which the officer in command was expected, with the inadequate means at his disposal, to carry on sharp, secret, and decisive operations:—

'New Plymouth: May 15, 1860.

'Sir,—I have the honour to inform you that on the occasion of my recent visit at my station, at the Warea, I have availed myself of the opportunity it afforded me for visiting the native forest pah, situated in the more immediate neighbourhood of that locality, and which, as you are aware, forms one of the three different pahs, or strongholds, of the Taranaki tribe, which have been erected by them since their defeat at, and their return from, Waireka.

'As in all probability it may be interesting to you to obtain from an eye-witness a somewhat more precise and exact view than it is otherwise easy to obtain, respecting the site and description of either (if not all) of the three pahs now extant in the Taranaki district, I take the liberty of submitting to you the following brief statement of what I have seen.

'The Warea Forest pah (the only one I have as yet found an opportunity to approach and to enter) is situated at a distance of about four or five miles from off the coast inland, in the midst of a dense and, as it appears, almost interminable, of what may perhaps be termed, light forest (i.e. of no heavy timber), on the summit of a small hill, called Mahainui, which at its base covers, perhaps, about one acre, whilst it is of so moderate a height as to render the pah (as far as I was able to discover it) altogether indiscernible from any distance (owing to the woody and undulating country by which it is surrounded), except within about 200 paces of it, more or less; all around up to its very base, the hill is surrounded by the thick forest, whilst the slope of the hill is cleared of bush, and rendered smooth, and more steep, by the red earth which has been thrown up out of the interior earthworks of the pah, previous to the erection of the outer double rows of strong palisade fences. Just upon the immediate edge above the hill, and without allowing any landing to take a footing upon, is the outer stockade or double row of palisade fence erected, which have the usual appurtenances for preventing their being scaled from without. Through a narrow entrance through the outer stockade you arrive at a sort of terrace of about eight or ten feet deep, the whole of which has been converted into what might be termed a deep or broad moat, and this again is subdivided by strong banks of earth and fern into square compartments—say 8 by 8, or 10 by 10 feet, and all of which communicate with each other by a narrow cut through the embankments (on the innermost part) that divide them. In these holes are the covered galleries, from under which the natives fire upon their assailants; and above them there are fighting stages, &c., to defend the upper part of the stockades.

'Having passed through the outer stockade and the earthworks inside of it, as just described, you reach the second terrace of the hill, which at the same time forms its summit, and the surface of which has much the form of a basin, being concave, and which is again, upon its outer edge, surrounded by a very strong palisade and fence. This forms the inner pah, where the women and children chiefly are kept. About in the centre of it, I observed what appeared much like a companion-way on board ship, and looking down into it I saw what seemed to me to be a strong subterranean vault, and a retreat against anything that might come in overhead, such as shot or shell. I would have been glad to have gone down into it, but this, and also making more particular enquiries, would have only raised suspicion, more than I am suspected already, and would therefore have led to no more satisfactory result; but, even as it is, I have seen sufficient to convince me that, in my humble judgement, the pah as it stands and is, is such that both the attack upon it and the taking it cannot fail proving to be a very severe task, and one connected with immense difficulties and considerable loss of life. At all events, it is by far the strongest and best defended of all native pahs

I have ever yet had an opportunity to see. Now a few words about the road that leads to it. The road takes its starting-point at the Warea village, recently destroyed; from thence it leads straight inland through an open fern country, only here and there approached by some small bush of koromiko, and very level for about a distance of two miles. At the end of this first part of the way begins the more woody part of the country, and the road, hard and level as before, passes through between plantations interspersed here and there, but all backed in the rear on both sides, by thick and dense bush and forest, affording every shelter and lurking-places to ambuscades. Thus it may be about one mile or more, when the road, which is thus far wide enough for a cart to pass, suddenly closes in with strong bush and woodland, so as to leave only a very narrow footpath to proceed on; and this continues all the way, say about two miles farther (with but one trifling little spot from which you can see nothing but trees all around you) to the very foot of the stronghold, through a forest as thick and dense with underwood as hardly to allow a cat to get through it, though natives (and perhaps they only) can make way through it. At all events it would require a road to be cut through it before any number of men, or more especially any artillery, could advance through it.

'Further, in the very thickest of this road it is divided by the Kpikaparea River, a river certainly of no great consequence; still, just where it is to be forded, there it would, as far as I am able to judge, require either to have some bulky rocks blasted, which obstruct the passage, or else the cannon &c. would have to be dismounted and carried through, and all this in the midst of, and surrounded by, an interminable forest, and more or less broken surface of country, swarming everywhere and in all directions with native skirmishers and ambuscades (who, being on the ground they are grown upon, and thoroughly familiar with, would have great advantages over approaching strangers), and without, perhaps, of affording any clear and eligible spot (at least, I could discover none from among the trees) from which to bring cannon to bear upon the pah.

'As I have stated already, the thick woods reach to the very base of the hill on which the pah stands, and surrounds it on all sides, whilst the sides of the hill are cleared, so that, in order to make an attack upon it, our forces would have to undergo a most murderous fire; and, in the attempt of surrounding it, either to breach or undermine it, they would by day, and more especially by night, be harassed by hostile native hordes infesting the forest all around.

'Allow me, Sir, to add a remark which I extract from a letter I have just lately written to a friend, and which runs thus:—"I do believe the Commander of the Forces has exercised a very sound judgement in not marching at all up to the pah with the forces &c. at present at his disposal."

'The number of fighting men collected in the stronghold may amount to about a hundred or upwards, but immediately they see danger approaching (and they have their spies out always) they obtain assistance from the other pahs; so it has been on your late going down there.

'When you went first to the neighbourhood of the Wareatea Pah, nine miles this side that of Warea, the other pahs sent at once, through the back bush, their men as reinforcements; and so Warea received the same when you got down as far as there; and on your return from thence you were followed up by the people from Warea and Upper Taranaki as far back as the Wareatea Pah, as they suspected that there an attack might be made, and other reinforcements had been sent for from

Ngatiruanui, and were afterwards only countermanded.

'Another consideration is that the natives, if it comes to close quarters upon them, and after they might have harassed and cut off many of our brave troops on the road to the pahs, will in all probability evacuate the pah before it could possibly be surrounded and closed in, and retreat to another one, about ten or eighteen miles farther off, and there try the game over again.

'I must close in hurry, for the present time permits no more.

'I have, &c.,

(Signed) 'J. L. REIMENSCHNEIDER.

'To the Hon. Colonel Gold,
Commander of the Forces.'

From this letter the reader will easily comprehend some of the difficulties that must be encountered in carrying on a war in New Zealand.

New Plymouth contained at this time,

in addition to its male population, about 1,700 women and children. The actual position of the enemy was difficult to ascertain. William King's strongholds and places of retreat would certainly be Mataitawa, Manutahi, and Kairan—places near the Waitara, well embedded in the forest; and, in addition, he occupied Puketakauere, the pah unsuccessfully attacked by our troops on the 27th of June, and distant about two thousand yards from the camp Waitara.

The Taranaki and Ngatiruanui tribes to the south surrounded Omata and Waireka in detached bodies. Scattered in small parties in the forest between this and the Waitara, they could, under its cover, unite at a very short notice, and could break up again as suddenly—as indeed they often did, even before we had heard of their union. This was done with no apparent, and I believe no real, object in view, though it actually caused continual alarms in the overcrowded town. The natives who remained friendly to us were the husbands, fathers, and relatives of many of those in the camp of the enemy, and intercourse between the friendly and rebel natives could not be prevented. Those who still remained faithful to the English, did so because they felt that English power must, in the end, triumph over the small means at the disposal of the New Zealanders. Still, their feelings were with their own race, whose cause of complaint they believed to be a just one. The last success of the natives at Puketakauere had given many of them an exaggerated notion of their power, and led some of our staunchest friends to doubt if the reign of the Pakeha was not really about to terminate, and the Mäori again to become an independent nation; so that the whole country was ripe for rebellion, and very little was required to cause a general rising of the tribes throughout the northern island. As may be supposed, information from the natives was difficult to be obtained, and when given, it was given unwillingly; it was generally too late to be of any use, and was always neutralised by our plans and movements being communicated to the enemy.

The Native Department, which was not organised as an intelligence department, was the principal and best source from which to obtain information; and its officers ventured during the war into the interior of the country, and even into the very camps of the enemy, gaining all the information possible.

The Mäori, however, though glad to maintain some show of friendship with his old master and adviser, which might be to his advantage if the fortune of war turned against him, was too cautious to let anything be seen that did not suit him; and the daily and hourly contradictory reports that came in, while they created anxiety as to the progress of the outbreak, gave little information that could be depended on.

Another source of intelligence was from the missionaries residing in the Waikato and in other disturbed districts; and during the heat of the war, and up to its termination, these gentlemen remained at their posts in the midst of the most turbulent tribes, whose blood was inflamed by news of repeated defeats, and by the sight of their maimed and wounded comrades returning from the field. From such a source it was natural to expect that valuable information might be obtained; such, however, was not the case, and the intimation of movements was either old, contradictory, or too vague to be of any use. In addition to this, the missionaries had little knowledge of military matters; and, speaking from their experience of the manner in which our feuds with the Mäori had hitherto been conducted, they had overestimated his sagacity, his superiority to the European, and the inaccessibility of his strongholds against systematic attack.

There still remained two other sources from which intelligence might be gained, viz., from the settlers and those military officers who had been some time in the country. On enquiry it turned out that the settlers, located on their own farms and occupied with their own affairs, could tell little beyond the limits of their homesteads; and the few observations they could make in driving cattle, farming, and the other pursuits of their calling, were not valuable for military purposes. Officers had been discouraged from travelling into the interior, partly because the state of our relations with the Mäori did not render it safe, and probably also because the habits of the former would have done more to estrange than to conciliate the independent tribes in the interior; and in the few excursions that they had been enabled to make into the interior, officers appeared to have remarked mostly on the picturesque.

After-experience showed the Mäori that

his superiority to the European was a mistake. The advantage he really had lay in his knowledge of the country, and his aptitude, individually, to avail himself of its many difficulties; but as to his boasted sagacity and military genius, the positions he took up, the strong ones he abandoned, and the want of opposition made to the force, on all occasions, on its advance to the attack through an intricate country, where every inch could have been defended, and daily loss inflicted on the advancing party, did not bear out the idea of high military talent so generally attributed to him by all parties. No strategical knowledge was shown by the Mäori in his plans, and but little praise need be given to him in the mere selection of a place on which to build a pah, in a country where the difficulty was to find a bad one. One principle, however, he maintained all through, viz., that his escape should be secure; and no pah was ever placed on a spot of bush that could be surrounded, or in such a position that his line of retreat could be intercepted. The fact was, our repeated failures in former wars with the Mäori had been caused by our own blunders and want of system. We had ignored this, and had attributed our want of success to the superior military genius of the savage, who at last, taking us at our own valuation, maintained openly that he was more than our match.

The following extract of a memorandum by the Governor's Ministers, dated Auckland, April 27th 1860, bears out this view:

'The absurdity of these pretensions does not render them less dangerous. Unfortunately they are supported in the minds of the natives by an overweening opinion of their own warlike skill and resources. It must be confessed that the imperfect success of military operations in New Zealand has given some countenance to the natives' fixed opinion of their own superiority. In the debates of the Mäori Council a

Ngaruawahia, the experience of the wars against Heki and Rangihaeata, and of the Wanganui war, are constantly referred to as showing how little is to be feared from the prowess and the boasted warlike appliances of the Pakeha.'

Still the Mäori was by no means an enemy to be despised: he was a noble-looking, stalwart man, well armed, brave, naturally fond of war and excitement, and a patriot fighting for his country's independence. His clothing was light—usually a blanket, which in fighting was dispensed with.

The following letter from Epiha, the wife of the chief who commanded the tribes at the Waitara, on hearing of the reverse sustained by the Waikatos under his command at Mahoetahi, will show the proper care taken of their husbands' clothes by the Mäori women, and the small amount of baggage required:—

'Kihikihi: November 21, 1860.

'Go this my loving letter to Epiha. Salutations to you and to your fathers who are lost, and all your relatives. Their death is very bad, having passed into the hands of the Europeans. If you had recovered them it would have been clear in our thoughts, because it was you who moved them about.

'Enough of my sighing! Friend Epiha, salutations to you: great is my love towards you, because you escaped from death.

'I have a question to put to you respecting your garment. If you lost all in the fight, write, and I will send you a blanket.

(Signed) 'HANA EPIHA.'

The Native Commissariat Department was also easily managed. The women carried the food for the men on their backs, and to any distance, consuming little themselves. All the tribes converging on

Taranaki also adopted the plan of planting potatoes, &c. on the road to the seat of war; so that by these means they might secure food for their return after a few months; or, in the event of their requiring them, the crops could be raised and forwarded to the front. The sites of these plantations were quite beyond all reach of our operations.

CHAPTER IV.

New Plymouth fortified—Refusal of the civil authorities to aid in the removal of the women and children, and in sanitary operations, with its consequences—Plans for victualling the town—Selfishness of the settlers—Presumption and inefficiency of the Volunteers—The enemy abandon their pahs, and retire into the forest—Expedition to Burton's Hill, and escape of the enemy—Mäori tactics—Plan adopted by General Pratt.

IMMEDIATELY on landing, the Major-General proceeded to inspect the defences of the town and its outposts. For the former little had been done, and the latter were clearly on too extended a scale. Orders were at once issued to surround the main portion of the town with a parapet and ditch, or stockade, according to circumstances, and for curtailing as far as possible the extended line of outposts. The latter could at the time be only partially done, but the former was at once taken in hand most energetically. The defence of the town by an enceinte was at that time, and up to the end of the war in March 1861, much criticised, both as to its necessity, and as to the actual security obtained. It was, however, a very necessary measure; it gave a defined limit, beyond which people were warned not to reside or to venture. Those who disobeyed orders, and many did so, did it at their own risk; and most of the casualties that occurred to the settlers, all of whom, capable of bearing arms, were at a distance beyond these limits, where they had apparently gone for the mere pleasure of disobeying orders, and in defiance of repeated proclamations and warnings, and with no object in view but to look at, not to look after, their lands and houses, to which at present their visits could do no good. It made the posts of alarm more easily accessible, and enabled a chain of sentries to be kept with some continuity. It also prevented marauders from creeping through the numerous ravines, and setting fire to the wooden houses of the town. It is quite true that this work was not an insurmountable obstacle to an enemy, nor was it capable of resisting at all points an organised and determined attack. Neither time nor means were at hand, nor was it ever contemplated, to erect such a defence. It was, however, a good fieldwork, answering the purpose for which it was mainly constructed; and interposing with its ditch, and parapet thickly covered with broken bottles, a very formidable interruption—especially to savages with naked feet—in making a night attack. Had such an attack been attempted it would have given time to the garrison to get under arms and to repair to their posts, and to the women and children of the settlers to gain the shelter provided for them. The outposts encircling the town were block-houses placed on commanding sites, but they were used rather as barracks than for this duty, as the nature of the country quite precluded, with the small number of troops in hand, anything like a continuous circuit.

Alarms by day and night were of frequent occurrence, causing the women and children of the families still living beyond the prescribed limits to rush in confusion and uproar to Marsland Hill; so that it was clearly necessary to remove the greater number of them to some place of safety, farther from military operations. The Major-General at once turned his attention to this most disagreeable duty; and tried, by showing the exigency of the occasion, to enlist the influence of the acting superintendent of the Province and other civil authorities in aiding him to carry out his views to this end. Far from receiving that amount of support from the colonists (on whose account the war had originated) that he had a right to expect in carrying out a measure of this kind, he was met with nothing but difficulties, and when not openly opposed he was passively resisted. For the civil authorities declined to have any hand in a measure so unpopular, and left the obnoxious duty to be carried out by the military alone as they best could. They alleged that martial law had superseded their authority, and that they now had no power. The real fact of the case was, that the more influential persons of the district were averse to sending their own families away; and, therefore, had no desire to see such a measure carried out in its entirety. They were quite aware that the presence of their families in New Plymouth must hamper military operations and protract the war; but they calculated that the expenditure, from which they largely benefited, and the compensation which they anticipated, would far more than recompense them for the temporary loss of their homesteads, and the inconvenience of living in a crowded town. The whole subject was referred to the Government in Auckland, the result of which was an acknowledgement of the necessity for the measure, and to cause them to forward a very inadequate sum of money for the purpose, which was doled out most sparingly and grudgingly by the Taranaki civil authorities who had the control of it.

It soon became clear that under their arrangements no families would leave unless it suited their plans. In a sanitary point of view the town could not contain its numerous inhabitants without a risk of engendering much disease; and though the heavy rains that now fell cleared the half-formed streets of much refuse, still the want of drainage and the accumulation of filth in houses crowded with families living in dirt and discomfort, rendered it too probable that the consequences would be most disastrous when the hot and dry season should set in. As it was, fevers and diphtheria pervaded the town when the hot season did come; even although some hundreds of women and children had with great difficulty been removed, and the garrison had been reduced by the force sent to the Waitara; and even although the Deputy Inspector-General of Hospitals had aroused the better class to their danger, and showed them the urgent necessity for drainage and cleansing.

Many lives were sacrificed, owing to the ignorance and obstinacy of the people in not attending to his sanitary regulations. For, while disease and death were rife among the families in the town, the soldiers in the same place were most healthy; and in the outposts and at the more distant camp at the Waitara, disease was unknown. Had the original numbers remained in New Plymouth, the mortality would, probably, have been fearfully great.

On the 22nd of August the Major-General embarked in the 'Victoria' for Auckland, to concert with His Excellency the best means of bringing the war to a successful termination, and to urge forcibly on the Government the necessity of its taking decided steps in removing those who now encumbered the town and prevented all distant military operations; and, if possible, to induce it to give the requisite pecuniary aid to the Province—the unfortunate scene of war—that the distress consequent on temporary banishment from their homes might be alleviated.

The Government, however, afforded only the most lukewarm assistance in this matter; contenting themselves with merely granting him an indemnity for any steps he might take, and with placing a steamer at his disposal for a few trips, instead of sending some person to the spot armed with authority and supplied with funds sufficient for the purposes required.

With much trouble and difficulty about 600 women and children were eventually removed to Nelson. The opposition, however, was very great, and the encouragement to resist given by the civil authorities, and by the richer portion of the inhabitants, who mostly held commissions in the local corps, was very decided. It was found impossible to remove any more without resorting to the employment of actual force, which was not desirable. The remainder of the inhabitants were therefore left to endure whatever might be the consequences of their own folly. And on the 8th September the General reported to His Excellency that he had done all that he considered advisable with regard to moving the families.

Early in the month of August General Pratt visited the camp at the Waitara, and reconnoitred the enemy's position; and, leaving instructions for the preparations for his contemplated attack, returned to New Plymouth to hurry on the defences there. These were pushed on during the next few days, interrupted by occasional alarms and by skirmishes with small parties of the rebels who showed on the edge of the main forest. These were, however, only marauding parties, burning the more distant and deserted farm-houses.

The population of the district had been obliged to leave their lands uncultivated, and to flock into a confined town; it was clear that vegetables, milk and other necessary articles of consumption would soon become scarce. To obviate this result every aid was offered to the settlers * to cultivate

---

'Superintendent's Office: 19th October 1860.

* 'Major-General Pratt having approved of a plan whereby settlers may cultivate their farms in the neighbourhood of military posts, the following conditions relating thereto are published for general information; and all persons who may desire to avail themselves of the opportunity for raising such crops as the season admits of, should at once make application at this office.

'1. The farms should be in blocks, to enable the persons cultivating the land to work together and protect each other.

'2. A farm-building, in which the labourers would

their land, by converting suitable residences into block-houses, by establishing codes of signals, &c. By this system of outposts, from which no military duty but self-defence was required, it was intended to keep the enemy confined to his forest while the farmer sowed his crops. This plan, which was proposed by the Major-General, and some time after again suggested by the Commanding Royal Engineer, was not tried because the settlers did not feel secure without more permanent military protection; and because they all thought their own houses and their own lands were those which should

reside, will be selected for the purpose of being fortified. Materials for doing so will be found, but the persons themselves must give the requisite labour.

'3. The persons so combining together will be relieved from the present military duty whilst so employed, but they must live together in the building to be selected, for mutual protection and defence.

'(Signed) E. L. Humphries.'

Taranaki Herald, Nov. 10th, 1860.

be especially chosen to be benefited by being saved and cultivated at the public expense. None of them cared for the general good. The plan eventually adopted, and by which much valuable food was supplied to families in the town, was to cultivate a large reserve close to the lines. To do this it first required to be fenced in. A native corps had been formed and was employed on this duty, with orders to clear away useless bush, but not to cut down any ornamental wood, the property of the colonists. This, though an advantage to the settlers, who before the war would have been only too glad to have had their land cleared without expense, was now objected to by them; and compensation was claimed for the damage done. They even proposed that all the wood required for this purpose should be cut on the lands belonging to the natives, and that it should be cut by the natives themselves without payment!

Another source of difficulty was found

in dealing with the newly raised local corps. They imagined themselves fitted for every emergency, and equal, if not superior, to the regular troops. The officer commanding the militia and volunteer corps solicited an audience with the General for himself and the captains of the volunteer companies; and at this interview these gentlemen explained that their knowledge of the country, gained by a long residence in it, had rendered them far better fitted to carry on a war with the natives than it was possible for soldiers to be; and they requested that the Major-General would strike them off garrison duty for a time, in order that they might carry on a guerilla war on their own lands, asserting that in a few weeks not a Mäori should be seen in the district. As there was at the time no immediate prospect of bringing the natives to action, and as he had no wish to curb such patriotic zeal, the General assented to the proposition. The weather suddenly becoming very boisterous the volunteers were unable to commence operations. During the storms, however, the brig 'George Henderson' was wrecked on the coast; and as it was presumed that the natives would come down to plunder it, two or three ambuscades were laid, but without effect. Beyond this no move was made, no organised plan was adopted, nor were any steps taken likely to obtain the promised result. As the volunteers still remained in the town, notwithstanding that the weather cleared up, the officer commanding them was called on to explain, when it appeared that the men were not willing to undertake the duty proposed for them by their officers. The scheme then fell to the ground, and the corps were ordered to resume garrison duties.

The works were continued during the absence of the Major-General at Auckland, and no event of any moment, on either side, took place until the 27th of August, when

Major Hutchins, 12th Regiment, commanding at Waireka, sent in word that the enemy had abandoned their positions there, and that he had destroyed them. They were found to consist of covered rifle-pits on the slope of the hill, in double and treble lines, flanked by stockades, traversed and having passages of retreat to the rear. This unexpected step on the part of the natives enabled General Pratt, on his return to New Plymouth, on the 28th, to do what he had always been most anxious to do, viz. to withdraw the outpost at the Waireka, without risking an action in which much loss of life on our side must have occurred, and the result of which could at most have been the capture of a post which must have been abandoned the next day—a conquest that could have had no influence on the issue of the war, which was to be decided on the north and not on the south of New Plymouth.

On the 29th information was received

from the Waitara that the enemy had abandoned the Puketakauere Pah, which our troops had then destroyed. Thus the enemy had given up their lines of defence to the north and to the south, and had retired into the forest, whence they issued in small parties by day and night, and burnt the deserted wooden tenements of the settlers, and drove off their cattle with impunity. Many of the buildings were in the forest itself, quite beyond our protection, as also were the cattle, which were scattered over an unfenced district. Escorts were freely offered to the settlers to drive their cattle into the town that they might be sold to the contractors. But, though the contractors offered about double what the colonists had been before receiving, still, in most cases, they preferred having their cattle stolen by the natives, to losing the chance of the large compensation they anticipated at the end of the war.

Mr. M'Lean, the native secretary, who, during the short period he was enabled to remain in the district afforded much valuable aid, both by his influence and by his information, obtained intelligence on the 3rd September that a body of the enemy from William King's and the Taranaki tribes, had established themselves and were erecting a pah at a place known as Burton's Hill, about six miles from Omata. It was therefore determined to try and surround them. For this purpose three parties, averaging 250 rank and file each, started at midnight to take up positions: two to intercept the enemy on the lines of retreat that he would most likely adopt, and the third to advance on his position by daybreak. As far as Omata the road lay through a difficult fern country, but was well known to us; beyond Omata, where it entered the dense and impracticable forest, we knew only little of it. Notwithstanding any precautions that might be taken, a very few natives could have lain hid in this forest and could have fired on the column without being seen. The march, however, was conducted with the greatest secrecy and quiet, and the point of attack reached without any sign of the Mäori. But though the information was ascertained to have been correct, yet the enemy had escaped. The foundations of a pah had been dug, and building materials had been collected. Recently cooked food found on the spot showed that the position had been abandoned in haste. This day's march confirmed Mr. Reimenschneider's description of a New Zealand forest, and showed us how little persons who talked of flying columns knew of the country.

In a war against savages the European has at all times great difficulties to contend against; and in New Zealand, and more especially in a district like the one to which operations were now necessarily confined, this was peculiarly apparent. In all former feuds between the European and the Mäori the tactics of the latter had been to keep the war at a distance from their homes and cultivations; to take up positions naturally strong, the only value of which was that they were difficult of access; to cause much loss of life to the attacking party in its advance; to retreat and to vacate the post without coming to close quarters. By these measures they usually inflicted heavy losses on us and sustained little themselves. The same tactics were still adopted, though on a more extended scale, owing to their supply of arms and ammunition being now much increased. None of the positions taken up by the natives were of the slightest importance to them or to us. They did not cover magazines, roads, or any points of consequence; they were selected simply as spots the most inaccessible that could be found, from which retreat was secure. The abandonment of the pahs after they had answered their purpose, was part of their system of war. In the native mind victory remained with the side that lost fewest men, and not with the possession of the barren piece of ground on which the fight took place. The Mäori knew that when they assembled we had no choice but to attack them, and that we were only too glad when they took up a position. The mode of attack, however, was in our hands. Hitherto this had always been the same, viz. a rush on the place, which had at best resulted in its capture, with severe loss to us, and with little or none to the enemy. We had, in fact, played their game. After one of those attacks the Mäori dispersed to his villages and boasted of the number of the Pakeha he had killed; while we, having hoisted our flag on the captured pah, lunched, carried off our dead and wounded; pulled the flag down again; returned home to glorify ourselves on our gallant deeds, and bury our dead. The loss sustained by the enemy was always over-estimated. Everyone secretly wondered what object had been gained, and what had been done to bring the war to a termination.

This was the regular mode of procedure during the continuance of former disturbances; it was hardly ever deviated from, and so the tribes remained unconvinced of the superiority of our appliances, and conceived no great opinion of our aptitude to put them to the best use. When tired of fighting they dispersed into the interior, to their own homes and cultivations, and tilled their lands unconquered. Thus the feud perforce slumbered until roused again by the insidious machinations of some turbulent Pakeha-Mäori, or of some interested colonist.

The history of our colonisation of New Zealand, and the constant recurrence of these feuds with the natives, made it evident that this plan of warfare—if such it could be called—would not bring the natives to submission and order. If this end was to be attained by fighting, it must be conducted so as to prove to them conclusively that we were their masters, not only in pluck, but in the use of the appliances at our command. It was necessary to show them that their strongest pahs, or positions of any kind, were valueless; that the forest would in time be no further protection to them, and that all could be taken with little loss of life on our side. One reverse, such as that of the 27th of June, or a victory in which we suffered much loss of life, would now have raised the whole native population, and plunged the colony in a war which, ending in the extermination of the native race, must have begun by the utter ruin of the northern island. By an extraordinary chain of reasoning the public, at home and in the colony, appeared to be inoculated with the feeling that to carry on a war with the native we should adopt his plan of warfare, and that we should meet him in the bush in skirmishing order. General Pratt, however, decided that to adopt this plan would be to sacrifice the advantages of our superior weapons; for, if we met the natives where men could only creep singly, and could not support each other in any way, the tomahawk would prove a more formidable weapon than the rifle. The issue showed that he was right, for he brought the war to a successful termination before the winter set in, and proved to the natives how vain it was for them to cope with us. The nature of the country, the habits of the Mäori, and the peculiar features of the war, did not admit of a strict appliance of the theory and rules of warfare. But it was not on this account necessary to disregard them altogether; and in the subsequent operations theory was made to suit the circumstances of the case, and plans were not made to suit theories; and I believe for the first time in New Zealand wars the Mäori was taught that neither pah nor forest would for the future afford him security.

The cry raised in New Zealand, and industriously circulated, that the capture of a pah by us without the capture of the garrison was considered by the Mäori a victory, was calculated to mislead. It is true the Mäori had no intention in taking up any position, and fortifying it as he did, to remain in it. If he succeeded in inducing the Pakeha to attack it, and in so doing killed many of our men, losing few himself, his object was gained, and he naturally considered vacating the then useless pah no defeat. But if he was compelled time after time to vacate his posts, and to retire deeper and deeper into the forest, having sustained daily loss of his own men, and having inflicted little or none on us, the case was very different. He was too clear-sighted not to see this. Whatever we might say he knew that he had been defeated at his own game; that his loss was not only men—a serious loss to the Mäori—but prestige; and it was in this way that the Waikato influence was so much weakened.

The dress used by the troops on all

active operations was well calculated for the service, viz. a blue serge jumper worn over the belts, in lieu of the tunic, while a forage cap replaced the shako. In winter they had the great-coat, with the skirts tucked up, cut off, or worn horse-collar fashion.

CHAPTER V.

Attack and destruction of the Ngatiparirua, Kairau, and Huirangi pahs — Difficulty of the country — The enemy retreat into the forest — Major Hutchins reconnoitres the position on the Kahihi River — Misrepresentation of the colonial press.

SINCE the evacuation of the Waireka valley and of the Puketakauere Pah by the Mäori, the troops in New Plymouth, Waitara, and Bell Block had been occupied in destroying the deserted pahs of the enemy on both banks of the river Waitara, and in the neighbourhood of New Plymouth. A large number were pulled down, many "wharées" were destroyed, crops were rooted up, and much loss was inflicted on the enemy. The Mäori, on the other hand, retaliated on us by burning the deserted houses of the settlers. The continual movements of the troops in the district kept the communication partially open; and, though the main road was never safe to individuals, the tribes were more cautious in leaving the shelter of their forests. The numbers of the natives in arms at the Waitara, including the Taranaki and Ngatiruanui, who had joined the former, were at this time estimated at about 1,700; but no certain information could be gained of their locations, or of the numbers in each place, till about the 8th September, when Mr. M'Lean ascertained with some degree of certainty that a body had established themselves in three pahs, Ngatiparirua, Kairau and Huirangi, in a level country at the entrance of a perfectly impenetrable forest, which covered the road leading to the Ngatimaru district. The information was that the hostile Waitara tribes of William King, reinforced by the Ngatiruanui from the south and from the Taranaki district, had occupied these pahs; that the Huirangi pah was in the forest, and that any attempts to penetrate beyond this must be attended with much loss of life, and could result in no real advantage to us. We could hardly credit that the natives should be so emboldened as to venture to stand an attack in these pahs situated in the open country. But the information was trustworthy as to their presence there, and all native reports agreed that their intention was to fight. The only thing, then, to be done was to attack them in their positions and to destroy their pahs, and dislodge or, if possible, capture their garrison. To leave New Plymouth, with its imperfect defences and its crowd of women and children, without a garrison was out of the question; and a column of about 750 rank and file, all that could be spared, was drawn from the garrison and moved to Mahoetahi, a pah about eight miles off, belonging to a friendly native. They encamped here for the night, and all information tending to show that the enemy had determined on making a stand, orders were issued for the march. The strength of the force was increased by another column of about 300 men, who had orders to move from the Waitara camp by night up the left bank of the Waitara river, and to take up a position intercepting the enemy between Kairau and the forest. A column from the main body moved off at midnight, crossed the Waiongona river, and, following its right bank, took post to intercept retreat to the south. Both these parties reached their allotted posts before daybreak, at which time the main body, not much numerically stronger, but encumbered with the ammunition, artillery, &c., reached its post and advanced on the pahs. And then we discovered how little the country was known by the resident authorities and persons on whom we depended for information. Instead of finding a plain level country, easily traversed, as we had been led to expect, we found undulating ground, situated between two parallel rivers, intersected at right angles by innumerable gullies, at all times marshy and often impassable, the whole hid and covered by a tangle of fern and bramble from five to eight feet high. Through this the advance was led by a line of skirmishers of the 65th Regiment,* men who had been many years in the colony, and understood the nature of the work before them; and a fine sight it was to see them skirmishing through this difficult ground. As day dawned and the pahs appeared in sight all the troops were in position, and the situation of the right

* The natives never once ventured to harass any column marching through the district, nor did they on this occasion; but had they known the true advantage their country gave them, they could have found spots along the whole course of the road where they could have caused endless annoyance and confusion to the troops, and could still have secured themselves a safe retreat to the forest, which was not above two miles off.

and left columns was ascertained, but there was no enemy to be seen. A few shells were thrown into Ngatiparirua and Kairau, and the pahs were burnt. They had evidently been vacated at the last moment, as food half cooked was found, and other signs of recent habitation were apparent. The ravines and gullies intersecting the plateau afforded too many openings for retreat to render it necessary to speculate how the garrisons had gone. And there could be no doubt but that their place of defence was the bush and the Huirangi pah, which rested on a deep ravine, its right and rear covered by the forest. A volley or two were hurriedly fired from it by its garrison, who then withdrew to annoy us from the bush, and to lure the troops into it. In this they partially succeeded; and one man, caught in the supple-jack and unnoticed, was dragged in and tomahawked before his comrade had found out that he was missing. An officer in command of a small party, misled by bad information, entered the forest with his men, where they were entangled by the underwood and separated, so that they could neither hear nor obey orders, nor help one another. The above casualty was the result. Fortunately more men were not sacrificed in this ill-judged proceeding. This was after the capture of the three pahs and while the men, previous to returning to camp, were occupied in destruction of crops, whareés, &c.

Nothing more remained to be done in this direction. The enemy had retreated to the depths of the forest, and the troops having entirely destroyed the pahs and cultivations, moved to the Waitara camp. Our loss was trifling: one man missing (killed), and four wounded. That of the enemy could not then be ascertained, but they afterwards acknowledged that they had lost twelve men. It was certainly a disappointment that a more serious loss of life had not been inflicted on the enemy. There was, however, no help for it. The broken country, covered with high fern and bramble, gave such advantage of cover to the native that, surround his position as you would, he could still find many paths to escape by; and, unless he liked it, it was impossible to bring him to action. Still the day's results were satisfactory. The destruction of so many pahs, the constant harassing by escorts moving about, and keeping the natives, by day, at all events, either in the forest or on its verge, began to work their own results; while the many alarms that had previously disturbed the town now in a great measure ceased.

The duties of his department now called Mr. M'Lean, the native commissioner, to Auckland, where the attitude of the Waikato kept the Government in constant alarm. Before returning there he however wrote as follows:—'The several pahs and strongholds to the north of New Plymouth being destroyed, and the natives driven into the forest, where it is impossible to carry on successful military operations against them, I have the honour to submit for the consideration of Major-General Pratt, that at present nothing farther can be done in that direction beyond watching their movements and keeping them off the open country if they should expose themselves.'

This was accompanied by some valuable information regarding the country to the southward. It appeared that the natives in this part of the district had many old pahs in which they lived on the road to the Tartaraimaka block, and that they had erected and fortified some others on the block itself. A short distance farther, beyond this again, on the banks of the Kaihihi river, the natives were also reported to have taken up some strong positions, and to have erected defensive works, which latter formed the line of defence that would be attempted by the Taranaki and Ngatiruanui tribes until the war assumed a general form, and until the tribes were united under one common head. It was not improbable that pahs had been erected in this district without our knowledge. The country was now quite beyond visit from Europeans, and the native tribes who had not openly joined the insurrection were not likely to give information; besides, the wood required for making pahs was cut in the forest near at hand, and they could be put up in the course of a day or two. The Tartaraimaka block was a fine, open, grassy plain, and though new well-built stockades had been put up there by the natives, it could not be supposed that there was any intention on their part to garrison them, or that the old pahs on the road were intended to be defended, or, in fact, that the enemy contemplated making a stand nearer than the Kahihi river. To reconnoitre this latter position, and to obtain information as to the country, landing-places, &c., and to destroy the first-named pahs, a small force, under the command of Major Hutchins, 1st Bat. 12th Regiment, was detailed, and marched on the 19th September. In addition orders were given to this officer that, as there were reasons to suppose that the enemy were strengthening a position on both banks of the Kahihi river, he should reconnoitre it well without permitting himself to be drawn into an engagement, and should ascertain its strength and the best means of approach to it. The whole of this duty was well performed, and after carrying out his orders and remaining a few days encamped on the Tartaraimaka block, to complete the destruction of the enemy's posts there, his party returned to New Plymouth on the 25th of the month. The camp at the Waitara was now strengthened by the Head-quarters of the 40th Regiment, under Lieutenant Colonel A. Leslie, who was directed to move round the Kairau plains to complete the destruction of the pahs captured on the 12th, and to keep the natives back in the bush. He rejoined the force at New Plymouth on October 1st, having finished the destruction of the posts and crops as directed. In the performance of this duty, on the 29th of September, a few Mäoris crept up, concealed by the high fern, and firing on the rearguard of the party returning to the camp killed four men.

These events were at once seized on by a portion of the colonial press of New Zealand, which was apparently only too glad to have an excuse for venting its spleen on the military. The reports given were so inaccurate, and the accusations founded on them were so palpably untrue, as to be almost unworthy of notice; still improbable and unauthenticated as they were, they obtained credence in New Zealand and in the adjacent colonies, and even a wide circulation in some of the English papers.

CHAPTER VI.

Expedition to the Kahihi river — Difficulties of the march — Encampment at the Tartaraimaka block — Destruction of the Orongomaihanghai, Pukekakariki, and Mataiaio pahs — Their formidable construction — Conduct and consequences of the expedition unjustly disparaged — Return to New Plymouth — Movements and strength of the enemy — Attack and capture of the Mahoetahi pah — Political results of this important victory.

The garrison of New Plymouth having been increased by the Head-quarters of the 40th from the Waitara camp (which was thus reduced to 250 rank and file), the following troops were put in orders to proceed to Kahihi and for the contemplated operations to the southward. This was the largest number that could with safety be drawn from the town.

FIELD FORCE.—NEW PLYMOUTH, OCTOBER 9, 1860.

Corps	Major-Gen.	F. Officers	Captains	Subalterns	Staff	Sergeants	Drummers	Rank & File	Remarks
Staff and Departments . .	1	2	1	1	6	1	—	6	In addition to this, the force was accompanied by 150 natives of the friendly tribes, under Mr. Parris, assistant native secretary.
Royal Artillery	—	—	1	1	—	1	—	35	
Royal Engineers	—	1	1	—	—	2	—	30	
1st Bat. 12th Regiment . .	—	1	1	4	—	6	1	150	
40th Regiment	—	—	3	5	1	12	4	200	
65th Regiment	—	—	1	7	2	20	6	300	
Naval Brigade	—	1	1	2	1	—	—	26	
Militia.	—	—	2	5	1	4	2	76	
Mounted Corps	—	—	1	—	—	—	—	14	
Total	1	5	12	25	11	46	13	837	

This force was to have started on the 2nd of the month to attack the strongly entrenched position, reconnoitred by Major Hutchins, on the Kahihi river. But heavy rain set in, rendering the rivers unfordable and the roads quite impracticable. The expedition was thus delayed until the 9th of the month, when the rivers having fallen sufficiently, the force moved from New Plymouth. The first day's march of about eighteen miles lay through a very intricate country, thickly covered with New Zealand flax, densely wooded, and intersected by numerous ravines. Sometimes these ravines had to be headed, at others it was necessary to make a descent to the beach from the overhanging heights. All these natural impediments afforded the natives every facility for conducting a guerilla war, but they never took advantage of them to harass our columns. On this march the Naval Brigade, overcoming apparently insurmountable difficulties of country, dragged up from New Plymouth an 8-inch gun, with which we hoped a breach in the stockade could be effected. The force encamped at the Tartaraimaka block (a fine grassy plain, the only one I saw in the whole district), and early next morning it advanced towards the enemy's position. The country here became most difficult; and though the distance was only a few miles, the crossing the Katikara river and numerous ravines offered so many obstacles that it was 8 A.M. before the column reached its encamping ground. The right of the camp rested on the sea, and the left on the Mangakuio creek, with an outpost on a commanding eminence a few hundred yards in advance. The commissariat department occupied the Parawa pah near the sea, on the right bank of the creek, and was protected by a detachment of the 40th Regiment. This position was about three-quarters of a mile distant from the Kahihi, on the right bank of which, and occuping a loop of it, at about eight hundred yards from the sea, stood the pah of Orongomaihanghai; on its left bank nearly opposite and quite close to Orongomaihanghai that of Mataiaio; and again on the right bank but a little more inland, and distant about four hundred yards from the banks of the river, stood Pukekakariki, hid from our view by a belt of bush running midway between, and parallel to, the Mangakuio creek and Kahihi river.

The camp having been pitched, and working parties having been employed in completing a breastwork all round, two reconnoitring parties, of about 100 rank and file each, were sent out; one along the sea line the other up the Mangakiuo to see if the Pukekakariki pah could not be taken in reverse, and the enemy's retreat be thereby cut off. After advancing some distance along the creek, the fern became so dense and so interwoven with brambles that progress was almost entirely stopped. Moreover the numerous gullies with deep swamps running into the Mangakuio, all of which had to be headed, showed that road to be impracticable. The natives also fired on the party, as it advanced, from secure rifle-pits on the far side of the swamps and on the edge of the bush.

The line along the seacoast was, however, found to be good and free from obstructions; and near the Kahihi river a good view of the situation of the enemy's post was obtained. A clump of bush and underwood, not hitherto seen, covered the Orongomaihanghai pah, which it was now settled to attack first, and in this direction. At daybreak on the morning of the 11th October a guard and working party, in all 400 men (carrying gabions made and brought from New Plymouth), advanced on the pah, and entering the small clump of bush, arrived without opposition to within about two hundred and fifty yards of it. Here the intended line of trench was marked out, and with a flying sap the men were in a very few minutes under cover. The enemy had offered no opposition: seeing our advance they had apparently been expecting the usual rush, for which they were quite prepared by firing their volleys and escaping unseen down the ravines. It was not until 10 A.M. that they fired a shot. But from this time, and until near dawn on the 12th, a continuous and well-directed fire was kept up on the working parties in the trenches. The natives on this occasion, though not so numerous as they afterwards were, maintained, I think, a better directed fire—aiming particularly low, and just grazing the top of the gabions. During the night an approach was commenced towards the pah. On the morning of the 12th, when our works were approaching very close to the outer stockade, the enemy ceased firing; and suspicion having arisen that they had vacated the place by the bed of the river, a party went round towards Mataiaio on the left bank; and on a concerted signal an entrance was effected into both places, which were found to have been just deserted. Pukekakariki was then taken possession of, and the three pahs were destroyed. They were found full of potatoes, food, books, and other Măori articles; and from the pools of blood in them it appeared that some loss had been inflicted, though to what extent we could not ascertain; ours had been one officer and four men wounded. The success and good effect of the operations were undeniable. The Măori without inflicting any serious loss on us had been obliged to vacate a naturally strong position, and three carefully built pahs; all of which were of no value to him, except as posts in the defence of which he was to inflict loss on us. In giving them up without this equivalent he acknowledged his defeat. The pahs were all built of strong timber, braced together with supple-jack, through which the 8-inch gun, after a whole day's firing, scarcely succeeded in making a practicable breach. The palisades bound in this manner, though cut in two by the shot, remained swinging, suspended by the supple-jack, and were even then scarcely less formidable as a means of defence than when firmly fixed in the ground. The rifle pits were most ingeniously constructed, and flanked one another perfectly; while the precipitous banks in rear and on the flanks, affording footing to none but natives, had also been cut into small rifle pits. The whole of the pahs were covered with fresh green leaves of the New Zealand flax (*Phormium tenax*), in two or three layers, which, though they might not stop a bullet from the Enfield rifle at a short range, would certainly divert its course.

Strange to say, the capture of these pahs, which was looked on by the natives, from the little damage sustained by us in their capture, as a serious loss and a heavy blow to their cause, and by all conversant with

Mäori feeling, as a great success, was yet quite ignored by thė government of New Zealand;* and, on the ground that the garrison had not been surrounded and captured was even ridiculed by a member in the House of Assembly as 'the capture of some more empty pahs.' That in England among persons unacquainted with the country in which the war was being conducted such might have been the feeling, is not so much to be wondered at. But that in Auckland a member of the assembly should have endeavoured to affix such a stigma on the military is hardly credible. All persons in New Zealand know very well that to surround pahs in such a district is a total impossibility. They know that the enemy never dream of retiring through the open

* It was, however, the capture of these three pahs, and the description of the manner in which it was effected, that induced the *Times* newspaper to alter its tone, both as to the character of the war, and of General Pratt's operations.

part of the country; but that, unencumbered with a commissariat and the other necessaries of an European force, they slip out through the ravines, one by one, without regard to the main body, or burrow like rabbits through the high fern. It is patent enough that all strategical moves to intercept their retreat from their pahs would be vain. Nor could an actual investment of the pahs be made without more danger from their own fire to the attacking columns than to the enemy; and the latter in such broken ground would even then find means to slip away through some unconnected part of the line. After the capture of those pahs the Mäori confessed his defeat, and pointing to the forest said: 'These now are my pahs, I hope they are large enough.'

The prosecution of this success by an advance farther to the south was prevented by despatches received the same day from Auckland, with information that the enemy at the Waitara might daily be expected to receive a reinforcement of from 600 to 800 Waikatos, and that further reinforcements were on the way. Under these circumstances (the garrison at the Waitara Camp being now only 250 rank and file) it appeared most important that New Plymouth with its large population of women and children (viz. settlers' families 733, boatmen's families 91, soldiers' wives and families 86, making a total of 910), should not be left so weakly guarded. In lieu, therefore, of the projected move south, for which the troops had come prepared, orders were necessarily issued for the destruction of the conquered posts and the return of the force to New Plymouth, which it reached on the evening of the 13th October.

The news of the march, and of the unexpected approach of the Waikato reinforcements was strongly corroborated by native spies in the pay of the Native Department; their strength, the position of their camps, and many details of conversation held with them were most minutely described; and we really began to believe that the news from Auckland was for once correct. The camp at the Waitara was again strengthened, and preparations were made to meet this advance as soon as the enemy showed out of the forest. Meanwhile the site of the old pah of Puketakauere was chosen for a stockade to hold 50 men and a month's provisions, so that, if desired, the camp at the Waitara might be abandoned and an increased force be available for the field. As before, these most positive reports of the position of the enemy were again contradicted, though the informants had gone so far as to state the numbers that they had counted, the tribes that had defiled past them, and other minute particulars. One thing, however, was certain—that a move of the Waikato warriors to the south was taking place. Some parties of these halted to plant and to hold conferences, at which some spoke for and some against the war: some new hands joined while old ones left and returned home. The European residents in the districts through which they passed wrote most contradictory accounts of the state of affairs, and native intelligence could not be relied on; consequently there was no arriving at the truth.

One portion of the road from Waikato to Taranaki ran along the beach at the foot of a precipitous rock, known by the name of the White Cliffs, the descent of which could only be effected singly; and, in the hopes of obtaining information of the move of the enemy, a man-of-war steamer was stationed to watch it. The measure had no good result, and probably only obliged the natives to take a more inland route. By the end of October the stockade at Puketakauere was completed and, with a view of having signals direct from this new post to the garrison at New Plymouth, and to maintain the communication, it was intended, under the protection of a party of about 200 strong, to erect another stockade at the old pah of Mahoetahi. For this purpose a portion of the garrison of New Plymouth and also of the Waitara were directed to move on the 6th November 1860. But on the evening of the 5th, while a small party was repairing a bridge on the road between the Waitara and Mahoetahi, some of the natives showed in the broken ground, and a skirmish took place, with, as was long after ascertained, a loss of five men to the enemy. Late this night Mr. Drummond Hay, of the Native Department, making a most hazardous ride from the Waitara, arrived at New Plymouth with authentic information that the reinforcements to the natives from Waikato and the eastern districts had crossed the Waitara higher up in the forest, and that they had not only joined William King, but had, in force, occupied the old pah of Mahoetahi, which it had been our intention to fortify next day. The news was hardly credible, for the place could be of no use to them as a position. They could not expect to be allowed to remain there, and it was one of the few comparatively open places in the district.

The following letter was sent in to New Plymouth, to one of the native commissioners:—

'To Mr. Parris.

'Pukekoke: November 1, 1860.

'Friend, I heard your work: come to fight with me, that is very good. Come inland, and let us meet each other. Fish* fight at sea! Come inland, and let us stand on our feet. Make haste, don't prolong it. That is all I have to say to you. Make haste!

'From Witini Taiporutu, Porohuru, and from all the Chiefs of the Ngatihauna and Waikato.'

* This was in allusion to the steamer sent to watch at the White Cliffs.

The strength of the enemy at the Waitara was variously computed; but I think it would be fair to estimate it at 1,600 men. In a despatch, Auckland, October 2nd, 1860, I see the governor says, 2,000. They were mostly fresh arrivals, the flower of the Mäori nation, who had come down to join in William King's quarrel, not as his allies, but as his masters, to take the war into their own hands, boasting that they would now soon bring it to an end, and would drive the Pakeha into the sea. They most thoroughly despised William King and his tribe, as also the Southerners, who certainly were a very inferior race, and were treated by them more as slaves than as friends. And from the arrival of these powerful allies to the end of the war, what between English bullets, and the abuse and extortion of the Waikatos, the Taranakis must have led an unhappy existence. In their spirit of boastfulness and vaunting, the Waikatos would not listen to the advice of the inhabitants of the district; but the same night that they crossed the Waitara, they sent the letter above noted; and with a portion of their force occupied the old pah of Mahoetahi, the property of a friendly chief named Māhou. The position was on the direct line of communication from New Plymouth to the Waitara, eight miles distant from the former place, four from the latter, in the fork of, and not far distant from, the junction of the Mangoraka and the Waiongona river, about three miles from the sea, and about the same distance from the main forest, where William King had his head-quarters. The actual site was strong, a hill running parallel to the Mangoraka river, at about eight hundred yards distant, surmounted by two knolls, and surrounded by a deep and dangerous swamp, only approachable on one side, where a spur of the hill offered dry ground. The space between the river and the position, though comparatively level, was, as well as the whole of the precipitous bank of the river, covered with ti-tree, fern, and brambles, nine to ten feet high, and very difficult to penetrate. This cover might have been used by the enemy with great effect in harassing our advance. The news of the position taken up being well authenticated, the force previously ordered for Mahoetahi to establish the stockade was slightly increased, and two parties of the following strength were directed to move so as to arrive at their positions simultaneously. The column from New Plymouth, under Major-General Pratt, numbered as follows:—

	F. O.	Capts.	Subalts.	Sergts.	Rank and File
Royal Artillery . . .	—	1	—	1	17
Royal Engineers . . .	—	1	—	—	10
12th Regiment . . .	1	1	1	3	81
40th Regiment . . .	1	2	3	6	162
65th Regiment . . .	—	1	4	8	210
Militia	1	2	4	5	120
Mounted Corps . . .	—	1	—	—	20
Total	3	9	12	23	620

The Waitara column, under Colonel Mould, R.E., was composed of—

	F. O.	Capt.	Subalts.	Sergts.	Rank and File
Royal Artillery . . .	—	—	1	—	11
Royal Engineers. . .	1	—	—	—	3
40th Regiment . . .	1	1	4	7	150
65th Regiment . . .	—	—	2	4	98
Naval Brigade . . .	—	—	1	2	20
Total	2	1	8	13	282

The intention was to dislodge the enemy from his post, and, if feasible, to capture the garrison of the pah; or, if this could not be done, to pursue as far as the forest, and then to return and complete the stockade. The column from New Plymouth, having a well-known and good road to move over, about 7 A.M. reached the Mangoraka river, which ran through a deep ravine, and was crossed by two fords near one another. Here the natives could be descried in the pah, which was an old one, and was in many places open. The two 24-pounder howitzers were brought into position to cover the passage of the river, as it could hardly be expected that the native would forego his advantage, and not use the thick cover in front of Mahoetahi. Here, however, as on all similar occasions, no opposition was met with except at the very place where the enemy had selected to stand. The 65th then crossed, followed by the militia, and drew up across the main line about 300 yards in advance. The detachments, 12th and 40th, protected the rear and right flank until the main body, guns, &c. had crossed. Difficult ground had delayed the march of the Waitara column, which, on account of the thick scrub and broken country, could not yet be seen. The enemy now opened fire from the pah on the line of skirmishers of the 65th; and, about 8 A.M. the guns and equipage being well up, the order was given to attack; and the 65th Regiment, at the double, entered and secured the centre and east end of the pah, while the Militia, with some difficulty, crossed a part of the swamp and effected a lodgement on the west. The enemy still, however, maintained his position outside, at the foot of the pah and in the swamp and adjacent scrub. The 12th and 40th now came into action on the right, while the Waitara column, which had crossed the Waiongona, near its junction with the Mangoraka river, extended the left, and materially aided in completing the defeat of the enemy and increasing his heavy loss. Except from the puffs of smoke, scarcely an enemy had been seen; but from the direction in which these now appeared, it seemed that the natives were escaping through the scrub, and at last one large body, dislodged by some shells, rose up and fled. This, I think, must have been about the first of the enemy who had been actually seen during the day. An advance was at once made in pursuit, a portion of the force being left to commence the stockade. The enemy was closely followed up to the edge of the forest, and on the road, for some three miles, tracks of blood were found, and several dead and wounded were picked up. The loss to the Mäori was very severe; it was computed at about 100 men, and as 49 dead fell into our hands, and were buried by us, the estimate cannot be considered large. I believe the number has since been found to have been much larger. Those who fell, and whose bodies remained on the field, were all warriors of note, Waikatos, who considered themselves superior to the Europeans in New Zealand wars. They were well armed with good double-barrelled guns and rifles, many of which fell into our hands. The corpses that we buried were those of remarkably fine men, some of them influential supporters of the king movement. The loss of prestige was very great. The Waikato, who had never before acknowledged to a defeat—who had come to drive the Pakeha from the country, and who had crossed the Waitara on the evening of the 5th, confident of success—was only too glad, twelve hours afterwards, to gain the shelter of the neighbouring forest, leaving the bodies of his slain chiefs in our hands. Our loss was four killed and twelve wounded, mostly in the 65th Regiment, on which on this occasion the brunt of the day fell.

Colonel Mould, Royal Engineers, was left in command of the party to complete the stockade, and the remainder of the troops returned to the garrison at New Plymouth, preparatory to more extended operations.

The result of this action could not but be most important. Nearly all the tribes engaged had lost men of influence, and the Mäori expression was, that the chiefs of Waikato were dead. The suddenness of the defeat—hardly more than twelve hours having elapsed since the main body had crossed the Waitara—had also a great effect. The loss had been the greatest the Mäori had ever suffered at the hands of Europeans, while no corresponding loss had been inflicted on us in return.

Her Majesty's colonial steam-sloop 'Victoria' proceeded to Auckland with the intelligence of this victory; she returned again on the 10th, bringing the thanks of the Government to the troops engaged. But at the same time a request was made that 400 men might be sent from Taranaki (the seat of war) to Auckland, on which place the Government feared an attack would be made by the friends of the defeated Waikato tribes. Though to send these men to Auckland would completely stop all active operations, the demand was so urgent that refusal was almost impossible. The troops were delayed by stress of weather for a few days, but arrived at Auckland in H.M.S.S. 'Niger' and in the

'Victoria' on the 13th, on which date the Governor wrote:—'As soon as the news of the recent operations at Taranaki becomes known in the Waikato, it is more than probable that a large body of the tribes connected with the defeated insurgents will take active measures to avenge their loss. Indeed I have reason to believe that the chiefs in the Waikato are now discussing whether they will make a descent on Auckland or on Taranaki.'

The fact was that the Government dreaded the effects of the success we had gained. The Waikatos had been punished so severely that it was feared the tribes around Auckland would rise for 'utu,' or revenge. It certainly was a difficult and most singular position that General Pratt now found himself placed in. The Government, since the defeat of our troops on the 27th June, had been constantly urging on him the necessity of striking some decisive blow, and of gaining a victory which might enable them to make advantageous terms with the insurgents. They invariably ignored that, up to this time, he had been obliged to confine his operations to the Taranaki district, south of the Waitara, where the enemy was scattered in the depths and on the edge of the forest; and that to gain a victory, such as they desired, was, under such circumstances, impossible. The only thing that could be done was to harass and annoy the natives. This was effected by the constant move of the troops who had driven them back from New Plymouth, and they only ventured into its neighbourhood, to burn and destroy the more distant homesteads, when they could do so with comparative security. Above thirty large pahs had been taken and burnt, and much native cultivation had been destroyed. At Kahihi the enemy had been forced to vacate a position naturally strong, and fortified with much care, in which he had expected to inflict much loss on us.

Farther prosecution of this success was prevented, as has been stated, and the force was obliged to return to New Plymouth, in consequence of despatches from Auckland, which announced that the Waikato tribes were rapidly moving in force on New Plymouth. The report, though partially true, was not entirely so. The enemy were drawing to the Taranaki district; but, as had been seen, the main body did not cross the Waitara until the 5th November, late on which evening the first authentic account of their move was transmitted to the Major-General. The necessary alterations were made in the plan for the next day's march, and the enemy was met and defeated at Mahoetahi before he had time to establish himself.

Thus General Pratt, having apparently done that which the Government had all along desired, now discovered that he had gone beyond their expectations, and was asked to reduce his already too small force in the Taranaki district, and virtually to suspend all operations there, in order to relieve the fears of the authorities at Auckland, who, instead of now finding themselves in a better position to treat with the natives, were as much alarmed as to the possible results of the victory of Mahoetahi as they had been some months before at the defeat of Puketakauere. The problem General Pratt had to solve was a difficult one. All minor successes at a time when great ones, from the want of an enemy, could not be achieved, had been stigmatised publicly, and even in official quarters in New Zealand, as the mere capture of a few empty pahs. The necessity for the troops returning to New Plymouth after the object of an expedition had been gained, was described as a retreat; and false statements and opprobrious epithets were industriously circulated in the colonial newspapers to the disparagement of the General and his officers. And now that advantage had been taken of the first opportunity that offered, it was found that the success had been too decided. The General was not only to beat the Mäori, but he was also to regulate the exact quantity of punishment that the people of New Zealand considered good for him.

CHAPTER VII.

Military preparations — Expedition to the Waitara — Pukerangioria pah — Difficulties of the approach — Defeat of the enemy at Matarorikoriko — Mr. Wilson visits the Mäori camp — Strong position of the enemy.

On the departure of the detachment for Auckland, the strength and distribution of the troops in the district of Taranaki were as follows (pp. 140–41). The actual effectives in the garrison of New Plymouth hardly mustered 550.

From this time the most contradictory reports were circulated regarding the numbers and intentions of the natives in the Taranaki district; but it was clear, though they were concealed by the forest, that parties from all sides were flocking to them.

These new arrivals boasted of what they would have done, and how different the result of the action at Mahoetahi would have been had they been there. The apparently impenetrable position they occupied in the forest; their daily increasing numbers; the energy displayed by the leaders in the Mäori king movement; the opinion as to the rights of their cause—publicly expressed by influential Europeans; and the advantage many settlers reaped by the duration of hostilities, still kept the tribes united, and prepared to make a farther stand for their coveted independence. On our side nothing aggressive could now be done until the return of the detachments sent to Auckland, and until the completion of the stockade at Nga-puke-turua should place a few hundred men at the General's disposal. For to attack the forest in an effectual manner, keeping the ground as it was conquered, would require every available soldier in

DISTRIBUTION OF THE TROOPS AT TARANAKI, NEW ZEALAND.—HEAD-QUARTERS, NEW PLYMOUTH, NOVEMBER 19, 1860.

Stations	Distribution	F. O.	Capts.	Subalts.	Staff	Sergts.	Drs.	Rank and Fil.
New Plymouth .	Staff and Departments . . .	2	1	1	9	4	—	—
	Royal Artillery	—	1	—	—	2	—	27
	Royal Engineers	—	1	—	—	2	—	30
	12th Foot	—	1	4	2	7	2	167
	40th Foot	1	1	2	4	16	11	125
	65th Foot	1	2	3	2	24	3	166
	Naval Brigade	—	—	1	—	2	—	16
	Militia	1	7	10	1	26	8	378
	Total	5	14	21	18	83	24	909
Mahoetahi. . . .	Medical Staff	—	—	—	1	—	—	—
	Royal Artillery.	—	—	—	—	—	—	10
	Royal Engineers	1	—	1	—	1	—	9
	12th Foot	1	1	1	—	3	1	59
	40th Foot	—	—	1	—	1	—	30
	65th Foot	—	—	3	—	5	3	150
	Militia	—	—	—	—	—	—	7
	Total	2	1	6	1	10	4	265

Stations	Distribution	F. O.	Capts.	Subalts	Staff	Sergts.	Drs.	Rank and File
Waitara	Commissariat (Acting) . . .	—	—	—	1	—	—	—
	Royal Artillery	—	—	1	—	—	—	23
	Royal Engineers	—	—	1	—	—	—	8
	40th Regiment	1	2	5	2	10	3	239
	65th Regiment	—	—	—	—	—	—	3
	Naval Brigade	1	2	6	1	6	2	138
	Militia	—	—	—	—	—	—	16
	Total	2	4	13	4	16	5	427
Bell Block	Royal Artillery	—	—	—	—	—	—	3
	65th Regiment	—	1	1	1	2	1	50
	Militia	—	—	2	—	2	—	41
	Total	--	1	3	1	4	1	94
Omata	Militia	—	1	2	—	2	—	49

(Signed) JAMES PAUL, Captain,
Acting Major of Brigade.

the country; while to storm posts, capture them, and the same day abandon them, would only be encouraging the enemy to continue a strife that was carried on in the manner most beneficial to him. If the war was to be concluded in the district, without culminating in a general rising of the northern island, it was most important to take advantage of the dry season. The wet season would commence in April, the country would then become impassable, the embarking and landing of troops and stores would be dangerous, difficult, and most uncertain. General Pratt had written to England to say that if all the tribes in the northern island joined the insurgents, as it yet appeared probable they might, the next campaign must be in the Waikato country, for which at present our means were totally inadequate. Reinforcements in men and ordnance had been asked for— the latter as far back as May 1860; and until their arrival the war was perforce confined to the district of Taranaki, both because it was too late to transfer it to another spot, and because of the paucity of troops. During the short time that was left, however, the Major-General hoped that by a systematic attack in the forest, and by holding captured posts, he might ensure a series of successes which should induce the natives, who already showed some misgiving as to their power, to abandon a struggle so disastrous to themselves.

Preparations were therefore carried on vigorously to make the Waitara the base of operations. Provisions, ammunition, and stores were daily collected there, and as many carts and bullocks as possible were gathered for a transport corps. Supplejack, cut by the friendly natives at some personal risk, was sent to the Waitara in quantities, and the troops there, aided by the Naval Brigade, worked these up into gabions, of which a good store was prepared. The head-quarters of the 14th

Regiment having arrived from England on the 1st and 5th of December, the detachments sent to Auckland returned. But the weather, which up to this time had been beautiful, now changed, and the rain poured down daily in torrents, so that moving was impossible. Arrangements, however, were pushed on, and on the 28th of December the force moved to the Waitara to commence the intended plan of attack on Pukerangioria. The troops composing this field force were, when assembled at the Waitara, including the Naval Brigade and regular troops, as follows (p. 145).

The garrison of New Plymouth was thus reduced to about 400 effective regular troops, in addition to the Taranaki Militia and Volunteers, who, though detailed as part of the above force for active operations in the field, did not turn out for certain reasons of their own, and remained for the protection of their families. Besides these

FIELD FORCE.—WAITARA, DECEMBER 28, 1860.

Distribution	Field Officers	Captains	Subalterns	Staff	Sergeants	Doctors	Rank and File
Staff and Departments	1	1	1	6	1	—	—
Royal Artillery	—	1	1	—	1	—	45
Royal Engineers	1	1	1	—	1	—	39
12th Regiment	—	1	3	—	4	2	105
40th Regiment	2	4	10	4	30	15	466
65th Regiment	1	2	8	3	18	7	380
Naval Brigade	1	3	8	3	10	2	173
Mounted Corps	—	1	—	—	1	—	15
Total	6	14	32	16	66	26	1,223

there were the non-effectives who could be depended on for manning the alarm posts.

Pukerangioria, the right of the enemy's position, and the point on which our attack was to be made, was an old pah, situated on high and commanding ground, on the left bank of the Waitara, about five miles from the mouth of the river. Though open in front, its rear and left flank were embedded in the main forest, and the right rested in dense bush on a perpendicular cliff three hundred feet high. Only a small space in front of the pah was open ground, and up this ran a narrow path which was flanked by the forest and exposed to the enemy's fire. This approach for about one and a half miles was over steep and broken ground covered with fern and brambles, thickly interlaced and most difficult to penetrate; while gullies and ravines, crossing one another in all directions, sent their streams in torrents either into the Waitara or through the forest into the Waiongona river. Between these there was little space for the movements of the troops. At Huirangi the main forest, making a bend, stretched down to the river, and this portion of it, about five acres only, quite hid the position of the enemy at Pukerangioria from the camp at the Waitara. From the Huirangi pah to the sea the ground was level, though intersected with ravines and covered with the interminable fern and bramble, and with occasional patches of Scotch thistles, some eight feet high. This plateau was a large spur from the distant mountains lying between the Wanganni and Waiongona rivers. Its sides were steep and precipitous where they formed the banks of these two rivers. In the valley through which they ran, stood gigantic forest trees, the tops of which were barely visible from our position. At the mouth of the river, on its left bank, we had a blockhouse, for the protection of our stores and commissariat. The Waitara

Camp was on the same side, but about a mile higher up in the bend of the river; a large portion of its contour being protected by a deep marsh. Though the camp was conveniently situated, both as regards water and general requirements, it was commanded by higher ground on the right bank — under existing circumstances a matter of no very great consequence. For the tacit agreement seemed to be that neither side were to use this bank of the river; and even had the enemy occupied the place, our shells could very soon have dislodged them. The stockade of Onakukaitara was on the side of the old pah of Puketakauere, about 2,000 yards in advance of our camp, and that of Nga-puketurua was on the left bank of the Waiongona, protecting the crossing at the main track—known as the Devon line.

Early in December it was reported that the enemy had occupied, as an advanced post, Matororikoriko, a spur of the plateau near the Waitara river, midway between Huirangi and the camp; and that they were constructing an extensive pah there. The position was singularly strong. It was protected on one side by the river and marshy ground, in which stood a forest that was quite invisible from the plateau, on which we were, till its edge was reached. On the other side the only approach was by a narrow neck of land, only a few yards wide, which wound through interlacing gullies, covered with scrub and bramble. The spur on which the pah stood, running as it did parallel to the river, also gave the enemy a direct fire on the opposite steep of the plateau. The pah itself, as far as could be seen, was not very strong, but information had been given that the whole ground had been honeycombed with ingeniously-contrived rifle-pits; and that the whole length of the precipice had been cut into steps for riflemen. These pits were constructed with much skill; some of them were covered and well traversed, while those on the slope of the hill contained cuttings for escape, and had, in many cases, underground communication with one another.

On the evening of the 28th of December, the force was assembled at the Waitara camp, and orders were issued for the intended operations of the following morning. The plan proposed was to take up a position near Kairau, on the main communication to Huirangi, and to establish there a permanent post; and having effected this, to attack Matarorikoriko by a somewhat regular approach, similar to that which had been so successful at Kahihi. At 2 A.M. on the 29th, the following force paraded and advanced, strange to say, unopposed through the most adverse ground, to within about eight hundred yards of the pah (p. 151).

A suitable site having been selected, and the troops having been disposed so as to resist attack on all sides, the working

MARCHING-OUT STATE OF FIELD FORCE.—CAMP WAITARA, DECEMBER 29, 1860.

Distribution	Field Officers	Captains	Subalterns	Staff	Sergeants	Doctors	Rank and File
Staff and Department	1	1	1	4	1	—	—
Royal Artillery	—	1	1	—	—	—	20
Royal Engineers	1	1	1	—	1	—	20
12th Regiment	—	1	2	—	3	—	80
40th Regiment	2	3	7	1	16	8	325
65th Regiment	1	2	6	1	14	4	320
Naval Brigade	1	2	5	1	4	1	125
Mounted Corps	—	1	—	—	1	—	10
Total	6	12	23	7	40	13	900

parties were told off, and the redoubt, laid out by the engineers, was commenced. It was of an irregular half bastion trace, and had an area of about 2,560 yards. The work went on until 9 A.M. without a shot being fired; but about that time a heavy fire was opened by the enemy. The volleys were principally directed on the left face of our redoubt. They came from the direc- of Matarorikoriko pah, and from the rifle-pits in the adjoining ground, the exact situation of which had been hitherto unknown to us. The smoke, however, now showed us their position and extent, and how very near we had advanced towards the edge of the precipitous descent to the Waitara river. Our men worked steadily; the skirmishers, unrelieved, remained the whole day at their posts under a broiling sun; from 9 in the morning till 7 P.M. the enemy maintained a continuous fire on our posts, warmly returned. The Mäoris in the advanced rifle-pits were directed in their movements, and firing, by signals, from the flagstaff at the Matarorikoriko. This enabled them to fire with great effect, without unnecessarily exposing themselves. The work being now sufficiently advanced, it was garrisoned by the 40th Regiment, a company of the 12th, a small detachment of Royal Artillery, and Royal Engineers, and Naval Brigade, in all about 450 men. The remainder of the force returned to camp. The native garrison of Matarorikoriko, in a few hours, resumed even a heavier fire on the redoubt, which they kept up until daybreak. During the night, hoping to surprise the garrison left in the redoubt, the Mäoris crept up in the fern all round, but finding the sentries on the alert they did not venture on an attack. Work was resumed again at daylight (Sunday), but without any firing on either side, as the enemy hoisted a white flag. In the evening the 65th Regiment relieved the 40th, as garrison. On the morning of the 31st, when the troops were marching up to the redoubt, the Rev. W. Wilson, a missionary, who had long and lately been in the Waikato country, expressed his belief that the post was vacated, and volunteered to ride in and report. He was allowed to go, and received authority, if he found his suspicions correct, to direct a portion of the garrison at the redoubt to take possession of the pah. Mr. Wilson visited the pah, found it empty, and according to his instructions it was occupied by the garrison from the redoubt. The position was found even stronger than was suspected, and all available spots had been made use of for rifle-pits. The haste with which the enemy had decamped was evident from the tomahawks and "merries" left behind; and some hastily constructed graves showed that he had suffered loss, and that he could not carry off all his dead. Many persons maintained that we ought to have charged the enemy's rifle-pits, on the first day. An after examination of the ground convinces me that it was fortunate we did not do so. In the first place, the first line of rifle-pits was constructed on the edge of the ravine, and not sixty yards from our skirmishers, but the approach to them was covered by high fern, and they were invisible. Had we taken this first line, there were successive lines of rifle-pits, which, by a parity of reasoning, we should also have had to attack, and thus we should have been drawn on to storm the position; the very thing that the enemy desired, and that it was our special object to avoid. Secondly, had our men charged the first line of rifle-pits, they could scarcely have avoided going over the edge of the ravine, the existence of which was unknown to us, as it was completely hidden by the fern. Had this occurred the confusion must have resulted in severe loss; for the men would have had some difficulty in scrambling up the steep slope, and during the whole of the time they were doing this they would have been exposed to the enemy's fire from their numerous adjacent rifle-pits. Our object was not to take the rifle-pits, but to put up a redoubt; and I am sure that the effect of seeing our men do this, within a hundred yards of their advanced posts, regardless of a continual and heavy fire poured on them all day and night, had a most astonishing effect on the Mäori mind; moreover, it proved to them that we were going to retain possession of the ground we conquered.

Regarding the general plan of the attack, there could hardly be two opinions. By the plan pursued, the enemy vacated the place after two days' resistance, with a loss to us of three killed and twenty-two wounded. The enemy's loss never could be ascertained; but as we found twelve bodies buried, we may suppose many wounded and some dead were carried off. Our guns could not breach the place, and had we stormed it, we might and should have taken it in a few hours, but with heavy loss to ourselves and scarcely any to the enemy; for he would have slipped unseen into the ravine, when his position in the pah became untenable, and *this* he would have counted a victory. The Waikato however was humbled, and had now to submit to the taunts of the southern tribes on whom he looked down. This second severe reverse was a sad blow to his prestige. The destruction of the old pah was at once begun, and a new stockade was commenced and pushed forward. The fine fern trees which abounded at Matarorikoriko gave excellent timber for its construction, and was easily worked.

The Rev. W. Wilson now visited the enemy, who had retired to their second position in the forest at Huirangi. On his return he was accompanied by a fine young Waikato, who pointed out the recent graves of some of his relatives, which our men then fenced in. While it would not have been safe for others to travel about the country, the Mäoris always respected their missionaries; and though, as operations neared the forest, they declined to see them, they warned them off civilly, and never injured them. They told Mr. Wilson that they were glad to see him, and that they had only given up the Matarorikoriko pah out of compliment to him. This gentleman's visits were, I believe, principally with a view to induce the natives to agree to a compact by which they should bind themselves not to murder or to torture any of our men whom they might find wounded in the fern or scrub, or whom they might capture in any way. The Mäoris debated the point, and at last negatived Mr. Wilson's proposition, as not being in accordance with native custom. The matter being thus settled, they told Mr. Wilson that they could not admit him inside their position any more. He then left our camp.

The position now taken up by the enemy was very strong; his right rested on the

Waitara, and was on that small portion of the main forest that was divided from it by the road to Pukerangioria; his centre was at Huirangi, and extended thence, on the edge of the forest, to the Waiongona river, and was covered by marshes and by an impracticable ravine; the pahs of Manutahi and Mataitawa were on his left, and were in the midst of the forest. The whole extent of the forest was, for about 1,500 yards, one continuous line of rifle-pits, constructed in the usual ingenious manner, with passages for retreat. Their chief fault was that the loopholes, being on the level of the ground, caused their marksmen to fire too high. The Mäori now made a great stir to incite other tribes to come to his aid, and envoys were despatched south; and a large body of natives assembled at Waireka with the hope that, by threatening New Plymouth, we should be induced to divide our force, and consequently obliged to suspend operations at the Waitara.

CHAPTER VIII.

Construction of redoubts — Attack by the Mäoris repulsed — The enemy retires further into the forest — Operations against Te Area pah — Tamahana arrives in the Mäori camp — Increased energy of the natives —Truce granted — Arrival of the Governor — Negotiations for peace — General Pratt leaves New Zealand.

THE remainder of the 14th Regiment having landed at Auckland, furnished a reinforcement of two companies to the Waitara; and on the 15th January about 140 rank and file of the 65th Regiment from Napier and Wellington joined the head-quarters of their regiment, thus increasing the field force to about 1,500 rank and file.

For convenience the redoubts were directed to be numbered. No. 1 was that put up at Kairau. On the 14th a small redoubt, No. 2, twenty-six yards square, for one hundred infantry and one gun, was thrown up 600 yards in advance. The enemy, firing at a long range and high elevation, did us no damage, while we noticed that wounded were carried into the forest on their side. On the 13th another redoubt, No. 3, about 500 yards in advance of No. 2, and approaching the bush, was erected. During its construction a heavy fire from the artillery was directed on the forest, and the fire of the enemy kept sufficiently under; although, since the taking of Matarorikoriko, they nevertheless kept up a constant dropping fire, varied occasionally by volleys from different parts of the forest. On the 19th and 20th the troops were employed in enlarging redoubt No. 3, which was to contain 450 men. The ground in which the men worked was very favourable, but the soil alone would never have stood at the required slope had we not been able to strengthen it with fern. This was pulled up by the roots, or cut down close to the ground, and when laid on the space marked out for the parapets, and at right angles to its length, each bundle overlapped the other. Alternate layers of earth and fern completed the work, and thus a strong and nearly perpendicular and endurable parapet was rapidly raised. The whole force was always under arms, as it was necessary to watch the ravines, gullies, and the broken ground on both our flanks, as well as the forest in front. Stragglers were almost sure to be killed; indeed, two men of the 65th, strolling a short distance from No. 1 redoubt, were surprised by natives hidden in the fern. After this we discovered many places where parties of natives had lain to intercept stragglers; our men, therefore, became more cautious.

The system of redoubts necessarily divided the force, and as each redoubt had at least one-third of its men always on duty by night, and the whole of them skirmishing or working all day, the work was very hard, yet it was most cheerfully done.

The force from Waitara to No. 3 redoubt covered about three miles of ground, and was disposed as follows:—

Blockhouse Guard, Waitara mouth	50
Camp Waitara	390
No. 1 redoubt	450
No. 2 redoubt	100
No. 3 redoubt	350
Nga-puke-turua stockade	32
Onakukaitara	30
Matarorikoriko (incomplete)	114

Great excitement was evidently going on in the native camp, and it was reported that there was much dissension among the chiefs. Our steady advance, and the erection of strong posts on their own ground, hemmed them in closer and closer. This, together with the daily loss of a few of their number, showed the Waikato that if he was to maintain his position among the tribes, something decisive must be done. And it was reported that he intended making an attack on No. 3 redoubt, on the night of the 21st. The redoubts were in good order, well garrisoned and alert, and we hoped that the Waikato had at last been induced to leave the shelter of the forest. The night, however, passed off quietly; we heard nothing but the native war-dance, and the songs of the Mäoris in rear of the interior belt of forest. The next day the men were engaged in making an approach from No. 3 to the site of the proposed next redoubt; for, as this latter was to be erected in the forest itself, now occupied by the enemy, it became necessary to provide safe communication. At daybreak, on the morning of the 23rd, a most determined attack was made on No. 3 redoubt, by a large number of the natives, supported by their main body posted in the ravine of the Waitara. The attack was made principally on the left face, fronting the river, where the fern was highest and thickest, and the gullies numerous. The assaulting party succeeded in creeping up and establishing themselves in large force in the ditch of the work, before they were discovered. At half-past 3 A.M., at which time the garrison was mostly under arms, the natives commenced by a heavy fire from their skirmishers, on all faces of the redoubt, so as to keep down our fire while the storming party posted in the ditch rushed up. Colonel Leslie, who commanded in the redoubt, describes the affair thus:—'The enemy, in the most determined and desperate manner, rushed up the sides of the parapets, and in some instances seized hold of the men's bayonets; while others crept round the rear of the redoubt and fired into the gateway closed with gabions, or tried to scale the parapet, but without success, and suffering heavily from our fire.' Colonel Wyatt, of the 65th, commanding at No. 1 redoubt, directed a company of the 12th and one of the 65th to advance to reinforce the garrison of No. 3. The 12th coming up charged the enemy and dislodged them from the ditch of the left face, while the 65th went round the front face and drove them from that part of the ground. A 9-pounder gun was brought into play, which, together with the fire from the parapet, and from the 12th and 65th, completely routed the enemy, who, leaving forty killed and wounded, regained the forest, being pursued for some distance. Our loss was one officer and three men killed, and one officer and eleven men wounded. The actual loss of the enemy was not ascertained, but more dead bodies were found in the fern as we advanced; and as we approached Te Area, several newly made pits were discovered, each pit containing many dead bodies, buried with care and regularity. The Mäori never acknowledged to any definite number of killed, but having learned from us how many dead bodies we had buried declared that number to be his whole loss. Very many wounded were afterwards seen, and on the termination of the war the natives made a request that we would allow a native ship to take in their wounded at Mokau, a place somewhat higher up the coast.

This desperate assault on No. 3, though gallantly carried out, was not, as we afterwards discovered, what the Mäoris originally intended. It appears that their plan was to have attacked all three redoubts simultaneously. For this purpose three bodies of the natives were to have crept up in the dark, and to have surprised the sentries. The reason that induced them to change their tactics was, that while they were stealthily advancing, they observed that the usual watchword, that was regularly exchanged at Nos. 1 and 2, was not given at all at No. 3. This led them to believe that the watch at No. 3 was badly kept; whereas, the fact was, that the sentries had been directed not to call 'All's well,' for the first time, on the night of the 22nd; as it had been found that their doing so had attracted fire from the enemy's skirmishers.

On the 24th of January the sap was resumed and pushed on vigorously. The enemy, as it advanced, kept up a heavy fire from the rifle-pits, on the sap-head; and at the same time made demonstrations to the south of New Plymouth, in order to draw part of our force there. The supply of gabions was well kept up by the troops at the Waitara; and the work proceeded at about 64 yards a day. A small redoubt, No. 4, for a guard of 50 men, was erected on the 27th, and on the 29th an advance one, No. 5, for 100 men, was put up about 250 yards from the rifle-pits in the forest. After the establishment of this latter post the enemy's fire slackened, and in a few days nearly ceased; though natives could still be observed in their original lines of pits, or in others in the rear; but they gradually receded as we advanced. On the 2nd February the first line of pits was reached, and a redoubt for 450 men, two 24-pounders, and one 8-inch gun was commenced. It was completed next day, and garrisoned by the 65th Regiment, a portion of the Naval Brigade, Royal Artillery, and Royal Engineers. This redoubt was near the site of the old pah of Huirangi, on the road to Pukerangioria, and between the main forest and the detached belt that joined the Waitara.

The occupation of this post obliged the enemy to retire still farther into the forest, and to take up his third and last position at Te Area and Pukerangioria; but at the same time he did not neglect to take advantage of the broken ground and intricacies of the forest, to establish a succession of rifle-pits and ambuscades between the two positions. At the new redoubt, No. 6, we were separated from the main forest by a ravine, which, rising near Pukerangioria, confined the small portion of open ground between it and the Waitara, over which the main road ran, to a space of a few hundred yards. This new position of the Mäori had recently been considerably strengthened, and a range of hills, forming a semicircle to our right, and rising in terraces one over another, had been fortified with parapets, rifle-pits, &c., and their approach was covered by the deep ravine before described, passable only at one spot. As our right flank rested on the forest, which exposed us to daily annoyance, it was thought best to cut down the detached belt of forest — about five acres. This work was done by the troops in a few days, and a more secure road was made near the Waitara.

On the 10th February all the disposable force, 932 rank and file, paraded at No. 6 redoubt. The 40th took the left, the 65th, 12th, and 14th the right; the guns, ammunition, &c., the centre. The whole then moved to take up a position as near as could be done with regard to our communications with the redoubts. The country became more intricate, and the bramble and fern higher, and our progress was much impeded; for while breaking through these obstructions our men had to feel their way carefully to avoid falling into unseen pits. Still an advance was made to within about eight hundred yards of the enemy's position. Here, from the rifle-pits, no enemy being visible, a heavy fire was opened on the force. The skirmishers were thrown a little more forward, and No. 7 redoubt was commenced, where the head of the column then rested. The position was so close to the forest that it was absolutely necessary that it should be completed and well garrisoned the same night. By the most strenuous labour of all engaged this was accomplished by dark, and a redoubt having a perimeter of 240 yards, and an area of 1,650 superficial feet, was completed, under a constant heavy fire. As no one corps could be taken away from the other redoubts, it was garrisoned by a portion from each. Our loss was on that day one killed and eleven wounded. Though the highest ground for the redoubt had been chosen, the interior of the work was exposed to the fire of the enemy, particularly on the right flank. The same night and next day were occupied in raising the parapet, and defilading the work. The 40th then occupied it as its permanent garrison. Some old redoubts, Nos. 2, 3, 4, and 5 were now abandoned, the chain standing thus:—

Blockhouse at the mouth of Waitara	30	
Camp Waitara	585	Including the sick, wounded, and all casualties.
No. 1 redoubt	371	All effectives.
No. 6 redoubt	432	
No. 7 redoubt	435	
Matarorikoriko	60	
Onakukaitara	19	
Nga-puke-turua	31	

On the 14th, the redoubt having been sufficiently enlarged and strengthened, a sap, to run direct up to the Te Area pah, was commenced. With so few troops, distributed as they were over a chain of posts now extending five miles, the work was hard and harassing, but the men worked most willingly. The sap could not be proceeded with at night; as the rear redoubts, being deprived of part of their garrison, would have offered too fair a temptation for an assault, therefore the guard of the trenches and the working parties paraded daily at daylight, and worked till 7 P.M. A single sap was at first ran out, and a demi-parallel was formed as an emplacement for guns, its left resting near the Waitara cliff. It was defiladed from the enemy's fire by traverses. The works were thus pushed on till the nature of the ground obliged us to resort to the double sap, and, after an advance of about 450 yards had been made, a new demi-parallel was again added to protect the progress of the work. The enemy all this time were very active, and obliged our guard of the trenches and covering parties to be most alert, particularly on the right of No. 7 redoubt, where the long spur of the hill running into the forest, and separated from it by a torrent, was the daily scene of some sharp skirmishing, usually in the evening, when the enemy were able to creep up under cover close to our advanced skirmishers. On this spur, in the ruins of an old pah, we found a vault, carefully made, and lined with rough timber, which contained the bodies of many natives, presumed to have been killed on the 23rd of January, at No. 3 redoubt; or to have died subsequently from wounds received in the assault. The vault was opened, but it was impossible to ascertain more than that it was of a large size and contained many bodies, that had evidently been placed there only a short time before.

The head of the sap had now been pushed a long way in advance of No. 7 redoubt, and the sentinels kept a sharp look-out on it at night; but notwithstanding our watch some Mäoris, taking advantage of the fern and scrub, crept quietly in on the night of the 26th, and pulled down some 100 yards, and set fire to the gabions without being discovered. The next two or three days were employed in repairing the damage done, and in throwing up a small redoubt for a guard of eighty men, No. 8, within 250 to 300 yards of the pah, and the sap was again pushed on. A live shell was attached at night to the sap-roller, and so placed that if the roller was moved the shell would explode. But the Mäoris did not again venture into the works until the evening of the 5th, when an attack in force, and of more than ordinary vigour, was made on the sap-head, now nearing the pah. They were, however, repulsed with loss. On the 11th we had advanced to within two hundred yards of the pah, and gradually approached the cliff. This day, the chief, Tamahana, the acknowledged leader of the king movement, arrived in the enemy's camp, and sent a message to the General, asking a truce to enable him to consult with the natives, with the object of concluding a peace. News had arrived from Auckland that the mortars and Armstrong guns were at last landed, and that in a day or two they would be at the Waitara. Under these circumstances, and as the truce might therefore enable us to concentrate an overwhelming fire on some of the distant camps occupied by the natives, whilst at the same time we attacked the position in front of us, their desire was acceded to, and hostilities were suspended till the afternoon of the 14th. By that time the guns had arrived and were in position, and as the natives had not offered any terms that could be entertained, the works were again resumed at daybreak, on the 15th. No. 7 redoubt was enlarged to hold the battery of artillery, and a demi-parallel was run out to the left to the verge of the cliff, and into the enemy's rifle-pits.

On the night of the 16th the Mäori again attempted to destroy part of the sap, but the shell attached to the sap-roller exploded, and killed three natives. The ground all round the head of the sap was well strewed with broken bottles, which, together with the above ruse, probably deterred them from further interference with our works at night. The demi-parallel was quite within pistol-shot of the rifle-pits the enemy occupied, and the head of the sap now approached very close to the pah. Encouraged, however, by the presence of their chief, the defence became more energetic, particularly at daybreak and towards the evening, when from the front and right they poured in a continuous and heavy fire. The usual place for these skirmishes was in the forest, to the right of No. 7 redoubt, where there was a sharp attack on the evening of the 18th, the last affair that took place. Two officers and six men were wounded and three men were killed, before the arrival of the supports, when the enemy withdrew, having sustained a heavy loss. For gallantry on this occasion Colour-Sergeant Lucas, 40th Regiment, obtained the 'Victoria Cross.' This day Mr. M'Lean, accompanied by some influential Nga-Puki chiefs, arrived; and at Tamahana's request a truce was granted, on the morning of the 19th, to discuss terms. The natives appeared willing to agree to Mr. M'Lean's views, but appointed a final interview for next day at 6 A.M., at which time, however, hardly a native remained. Unencumbered with European equipment and necessaries, they had disappeared, and only a few influential chiefs were left to arrange all matters in dispute.

To occupy the pah, now that the enemy

had retired, was useless; and in native opinion it would be considered unfair. It was therefore merely stipulated that until the arrival of His Excellency, who was expected shortly, the few Mäoris remaining should retire from the front and live at Mataitawa. Some of our old enemies, however, came into the camp occasionally, and brought potatoes, pigeons, &c., in exchange for rum. They were very friendly, but were very guarded in their speech. On the 27th of March, His Excellency arrived, and negotiations were commenced that appeared likely to terminate in peace. On the 31st of March, while preliminaries were in discussion at a council, assembled by the Governor at the Waitara, Lieut.-General Cameron arrived with orders to assume the command in New Zealand. And General Pratt was directed to resume his command in Australia — New Zealand having been made a separate command. The command was handed over to General Cameron on the day of his arrival; and, on the 3rd of April, General Pratt sailed from the Waitara, in the 'Victoria,' having concluded the campaign against the natives; and having, in all probability, brought the war to an end.

CHAPTER IX.

State of the country — Review of military operations — Conclusion.

It was not to be expected that quiet and tranquillity could be immediately restored in the country, and that the Europeans could at once live in the distant and isolated districts away from the protection of soldiers or police. But the duration of this state of affairs would depend, if not more, certainly as much, on the machinations of the European community as on any actual ill feeling of the natives; and, indeed, it has since been seen that, so long as the English Government is content to maintain a large force of military in New Zealand, at the expense of England, there is no chance of the cessation of the repeated rumours of the renewal of the war, or of harmony being established between settlers and natives. Nor will the settlers, while they can retain this expenditure, cooperate with Sir George Grey to heal feuds and thus to cut off such a source of revenue. In former wars the natives had really lost nothing; and while we claimed the victory from capturing some hill or pah, that was of no use to either party, they could count their gain in the much larger casualties inflicted on us. They had now learnt a new lesson. From the arrival of General Pratt, in August 1860, until the end of the campaign, in March 1861, not a single instance had occurred in respect of which they could in the least claim a success; while the capture and destruction of some of their strongest pahs, the loss of many of their bravest chiefs, and the number of their dead and wounded left in our hands, were injuries that they could not hide or disregard.

And in the last three months' campaign at the Waitara, in a very strong country, peculiarly suited to their style of warfare, and one which they had selected themselves, they had not only been beaten, but the conquered country had been settled upon by us. Our redoubts had been built close to their own posts, and on several occasions within 100 yards and less of their riflemen. Both by day and night during the whole time they had been kept on the alert, and had been driven farther back into the forest, suffering a continual loss of men. The forest itself, when it interfered with our operations, was cut down in spite of the fire of their skirmishers; and the five miles of ground occupied by our redoubts became so secure that our people on duty rode forwards and backwards without escorts, and our ammunition, provisions, &c., passed up only slightly guarded. They had chosen this country themselves, their warriors were well armed, and they had ammunition and provisions in abundance. They were all animated with the feeling that they would carry on the same successful plan as before, and that when tired they could disperse. But in all their expectations they had been disappointed; they had been foiled in everything, and had to confess their discomfiture.

When General Pratt left, the winter was setting in. This season, when hostilities must of necessity cease, it was to be expected, would be employed by the natives in attempts to bully us out of concessions, —not that they could seriously contemplate renewing the war in the event of our refusing to grant them. They were too intelligent a race not to know how disastrous the struggle must eventually prove to them. They had seen that they had not the means to maintain a contest, even against General Pratt's very small force, that was opposed to them in the Taranaki district; and they could not be blind to the fact, that against the well-equipped army of General Cameron in the comparatively open country, they could have no chance; for, in the event of the war being resumed, they could foresee that the Waikato country must be the future seat of operations, in which case the Waikatos would lose lands, houses, in fact, everything they possessed; and moreover, their country, which they had hitherto jealously guarded from the visits of Europeans, would be thrown open to the colonists.

These considerations to my mind were almost a guarantee that the Waikato would endeavour to avoid further hostilities, unless forced into them by the impolitic conduct of many colonists, who, it would almost appear, are desirous of fomenting the quarrel, chiefly with a view to retain the enormous military expenditure, probably also with the design of exterminating the natives and dividing their lands; though they seem to have overlooked that this result could only be arrived at by a general war — lasting some years—in which the destruction of their property, in the first instance, would be inevitable.

The plan of the Waitara campaign, and the previous military operations of the war of 1860–1861, have been severely criticised by many persons who did not know the country or circumstances, as well as by many interested parties who did. It has been overlooked that one of the greatest difficulties was to find the enemy; for the Mäori was quite aware that his main strength lay in neutralising the efforts of our columns, by dispersing whenever we were likely to come to close quarters. It must also be remembered that there were certain political reasons for keeping the war in the Taranaki district; and besides these, no general with the force at hand in August 1860, and up to the termination of hostilities in March 1861, could have ventured to bring on a general rising of the natives. It is true it might have been done with this risk. In August 1860, when the colonists refused to send away their families, the general might have moved every available man into the field, and left New Plymouth and its inhabitants to their fate. Had this been done, however, the probability is that the soldiers would not have met the enemy, and that New Plymouth would have been burnt and destroyed by the natives.* And there were many even among the highest officials in the country who believed that, if the

* A very similar case to this did occur in the Affghan war during the winter of 1841. A portion of the force in Candahar was sent in pursuit of the Affghans who were hovering about the town. As soon as the troops had been drawn some days' march distant, the enemy disappeared. They had doubled back by mountain passes and short cuts, and attacked the weakened garrison.

They were repulsed after a sharp contest, in which they suffered severe loss, but in which they had first succeeded in burning down one of the massive gates of the town, and, indeed, they left many dead inside the gate itself.

Mäori did take prisoners, he would soon revert to his old habits and eat them. To have left New Plymouth, therefore, to be defended by its inhabitants, I consider would have been not only cruel but impolitic and unnecessary.

Without going back to the history of former wars, and reading the despatches of Colonel Despard before Heke's pah in 1845 with reference to his campaign, and without considering the causes of the failure of the attack on Puketakauere, on the 27th June 1860 (which occurred previous to the arrival of General Pratt), few who have seen the Taranaki country, in which operations were conducted, but will be convinced that they were undertaken on the right principle. The skirmishes round New Plymouth in August and September, the capture of the Kahihi redoubts, and the destruction of a large number of pahs in October, before the arrival of the Waikatoes, had even then worked a good result in the district. In consequence of our success, several natives who had seceded returned to their allegiance, and many more would have done so but from fear of the colonists, who treated even the friendly tribes with the greatest brutality.*

That the hill on which Te Area or Pukerangioria stood might have been charged and carried, though with much loss of life to us, I do not doubt; but, as has been

* One of these tribes occupied Fort Herbert, an outpost of New Plymouth, and on several occasions went out and saved Europeans who had strayed into the bush and had been attacked by the enemy. The prisoners we took had to be most carefully guarded, not so much to prevent escape, as to save them from the un-English and unmanly attacks of the Europeans, who, when they could do so with safety, treated them with the greatest indignities. Widely different was the behaviour of the soldiers, who, even when heated with the excitement of fight, willingly collected the dead, and buried them with decency, fencing in the graves. They also took as much care of the wounded on the field, as well as in hospital, as of their own comrades.

shown, it would have been just what the Mäori wanted. It should be remembered, moreover, that we would not have remained there, for there could have been no object in doing so. By the course pursued the native was completely checkmated. Had the Mäori nation joined all their forces together to attack us on open ground, as report gave out that it would, the war would soon have been brought to an end, and the native race also. I observe that this canard has, only a few months since, been repeated in the New Zealand papers. It was stated that 20,000 Mäoris were about to assemble with the object of attacking General Cameron's army! But who is to credit that the native, without organisation and without artillery, would abandon his guerilla mode of fighting, and all the advantages accruing from the nature of his country, to bring an unwieldy mass in front of our disciplined troops? The fact is, that this report was invented for the

English mail and the English public, with the sole object of keeping up the present large expenditure in New Zealand.

No better plan to destroy the prestige of the native and reduce him to submission could have been adopted. The belief of the southern natives in the strength of the Waikato was destroyed. The friendly natives in the district worked willingly, even at the Waitara, where, in proximity to the redoubts, they helped in clearing away fern. It was easy to see, from their pleased expression and altered looks, that whatever fears they at first may have had as to the Waikato defeating us and obtaining the district, these had all passed away, and that they were anxious to become entitled to be regarded favourably by the English Government. This and other circumstances showed, some time before the war was ended, that submission was contemplated by the insurgents.

The enemy's loss could not be ascertained, but we buried above 120 bodies on the field; and in our advance we found large vaults, where they had buried many more. The Waikato confessed to 400 killed in all, probably not half his loss. The wounded, known to be most numerous, were scattered all over the country, and were not likely to encourage the martial ardour of the more peaceable races.

Our loss, though small, was large for the small force engaged: it was caused chiefly by the unceasing daily skirmishes, in which a few fell every day. It was, however, nothing compared with the losses that must have ensued if the tactics of former wars had been adopted in this. It was as follows:—

NEW ZEALAND.—TARANAKI WAR, 1860-61.

NOMINAL RETURN OF THE KILLED AND WOUNDED FROM COMMENCEMENT TO CESSATION OF HOSTILITIES.

Corps	Officers			Men			Remarks
	Killed	Wounded	Total	Killed	Wounded	Total	
General Staff .	—	1	1	—	—	—	
Royal Artillery .	1	—	1	2	12	14	
Royal Engineers	—	1	1	1	4	5	
1st Bat. 12th Foot	—	1	1	1	7	8	
2nd Bat. 14th Foot	—	—	—	—	2	2	
40th Foot . . .	2	3	5	38	58	96	
57th Foot . . .	—	—	—	—	6	6	
65th Foot . . .	1	1	2	5	38	43	
Naval Brigade .	—	2	2	1	20	21	
Taranaki Militia*	1	2	3	11	16	27	
Total . . .	5	11	16	59	163	222	
	Killed			Wounded			Killed and Wounded
Grand Total. .	64			174			238

* Of this number only four were killed in action. The remaining seven, and many of those shown as wounded, received their injuries when off duty and straggling, as remarked at page 29.

(Signed) J. Mouat,
Deputy Inspector-General, P. M. Officer.

Principal Medical Officers' Office,
Auckland, Feb. 6, 1862.

The campaign ended on the 18th March 1861, since which time not a shot has been fired. The fine division under General Cameron has had no other occupation than road-making. Should war be resumed it could now be carried on on an entirely different footing, and on a more extended scale, the forces in New Zealand being now, for the first time, large enough to be called an army. Still, there would be many difficulties to be contended with that are not dreamt of in England, where the only feeling with reference to this country would appear to be one of astonishment, that a race of mere savages should not be easily forced into submission. Sir George Grey, who certainly is a good authority on such subjects, has a very different notion of the matter; or, at least, had in 1846, as the following extract from the New Zealand Blue Book will show:—

'The generality of persons who criticise military operations in this country appear to forget that there is no analogy between them and the military operations carried on in Europe.

'In that portion of the globe, if it is necessary to drive an enemy from a wood, it is with a view of advancing to some other position, or of opening the road to some town where supplies or quarters for the men can be obtained; in fact, the object generally is to gain possession of some tract of country which it is desirable to hold. Whereas in this colony, if the enemy retire into a dense and mountainous forest, of almost boundless extent, and our troops are directed to pursue them, the simple result is that the enemy are driven farther into the forest, and our troops are ultimately, after a heavy loss, compelled to retire upon the open country and their supplies.

'Indeed, the object has simply been to punish the enemy, and this could not be attempted under more disadvantageous circumstances than by forcing our own men into a position in which they fight to the greatest possible disadvantage, and the enemy to the greatest advantage.

(Signed) 'G. GREY.'

In this short history of the New Zealand war, I have purposely avoided speaking of individuals and corps of the regular army; not that I am insensible to their uniform courage, or to the arduous nature of their work. For months they were exposed to a harassing and unceasing fire from natives hidden in the fern and forest, and during the greater part of the time they were unable to take off their clothes. They knew that in skirmishing in the dense scrub, if a man missed his comrade and was wounded, he would be mercilessly tomahawked by the natives, should his absence be unnoticed when we changed our position. Their steadiness in the redoubts was admirable. When required to work, they stood on the top of the parapets within 200 yards of the enemy's rifle-pits, with the utmost coolness, and they occupied themselves with cooking, washing, and other necessary duties, as unconcernedly as though they were in barracks. All this had a depressing effect on the natives, who were unable to comprehend how men could 'fight and work together,' as they termed it. The quiet perseverance of our men, so totally opposed to their own habits, dispirited them beyond measure, and led them to doubt their power of tiring us out.

I will take the opportunity, however, of mentioning that there was one corps, the Taranaki Mounted Volunteers, who, about 30 strong, under the command of Captain De Vœux, did most valuable service. They were badly armed, and badly clothed, but they were well mounted, plucky, and always ready. Even in the most dangerous times they rode long distances, carrying orders, day or night, alone or in twos. It was with these mounted men that the communication with New Plymouth and Kahihi was kept up, as it afterwards was between the Waitara and the redoubts, where, anxious to work and ever fearless of danger, they were invaluable. One of them, Mr. Mace, an excellent rider, was the pluckiest fellow I ever met. I believe he lost much property at the outbreak of the war; and I trust the Government may have found some means to reward him.

Our land transport was very insufficient; we had only some 40 bullock carts, but with these we managed to supply the redoubts with ammunition, provisions, and gabions (of which about 60 were made daily at the Waitara), besides water, which was carted to each redoubt from the Waitara, and was kept in barrels. The troops will, I am sure, long recollect how much they owe Mr. Elliott, of Taranaki, for his exertions in keeping up the supply to the full wants of the men, under a good deal of difficulty, not unattended with danger.

In the foregoing account of the Taranaki

war, I have merely desired to place on record a correct version of the events that occurred, both because I conceive that the history of the war, when attentively considered, is a very interesting one, and because I have some hopes that my observations may tend to counteract the garbled and fictitious statements that have from time to time appeared in the public journals of New Zealand. The reports that have been circulated through them must have had the effect of giving most erroneous impressions to the English public—as they have to the neighbouring colonies here—not only as to the quarrel which led to the war, but as to the conduct of the war itself; while the natural difficulties of the country, as well as the available strength of the military, have always been intentionally underrated by the interested contributors to these journals.

CPSIA information can be obtained
at www.ICGtesting.com
Printed in the USA
LVHW040424110522
718423LV00002B/465

9 783375 001285